FALLING IN FLORENCE

Joy Skye

Copyright © 2021 Joy Skye

This is a work of fiction. Similarities to real people, places, or events are entirely coincidental.

This one is for Mr M - Supporter extraodinaire!

CONTENTS

Title Page	1
Copyright	2
Dedication	3
C'era una volta	7
La bocca di botero	20
L'amore è cieco	35
A caval donato non si guarda in bocca	53
Un po' di gelosia	64
Chi dorme non piglia pesci	80
Prendi il tuo partner per la gola	94
Le conversazioni intime	103
Il brivido della caccia	113
Le passeggiate mano a mano	125
A buon intenditor, poche parole	137
Non è tutto oro quello che luccica	147
Mangia bene, ridi spesso, ama molto	159
Felice per sempre	168

C'ERA UNA VOLTA

(Once upon a time)

From: Peterwilliams@sublimeretreats.com

To: Adamflynn@sublimeretreats.com

Subject: Italy Product Trip

Good morning Adam,

Superb work on the potential acquisitions in Florence!

I looked through the information that you included in your previous email and there are some really excellent prospects in there. I have ordered them according to my preference on the list attached, based on the information we have for each apartment, but of course we need to see them in the flesh, as it were, so go ahead and set up meetings for next month.

I am currently interviewing for a PA and hoping to get someone in place by next week so they will be suitably up to speed by the time we plan to be in Italy to deal with things here for me, as it's going to be a two-week trip I feel it's essential.

Again, splendid work, your efforts are appreciated and I am looking forward to travelling to Europe again.

Best regards,

Peter

Peter Williams

General Manager–*Sublime Retreats*

Sofia felt sick. Enveloped in the oversized orange sofa in the grand lobby of 811 Main Street, she twisted the silver rings on her fingers as she waited for someone to come and take her for her interview. Shifting position slightly to impede the sofa's apparent desire to swallow her whole, she kept a grin plastered on her face as her eyes darted to examine everyone who came out of the elevators, looking for a sign of intent. The bright, bustling, open space had an air of efficiency, money and a miasma of lemon polish with new carpets.

She had a meeting with Peter Williams, the manager of Sublime Retreats, for the position as his PA. She was desperate for the interview to go well.

This job application was the culmination of months of fighting with, then cajoling, her parents, who could not understand her desire to do anything but work at Margarita's, the restaurant that had been in their family for decades at Galveston Seawall. She had to get this job, determined to prove to them that she could strike out and be independent, even if she did still live at home right now. She'd yet to have the courage to broach the idea that she might do anything else; she feared her father would have a heart attack at the mere mention of the plan that had been brewing in her mind for some time. If she got this job, the hour long drive each way would be too much for her old car. She would have to make the break and find an apartment within easy commuting distance. But one fight at a time...

She was brought back to the present by a tall, handsome man standing directly in front of her, looking at her inquisitively; he'd apparently said something and was waiting for a response. He looked to be in his late thirties, despite the grey flecks in his hair. With a youthful face and a pleasant aura about him, she warmed to him immediately as she took in his well-cut suit and impossibly shiny shoes.

'Hi' she said a little breathlessly as she tried to stand up, but somehow sank deeper into the upholstery. Smiling, the man stretched out a hand and helped pull her into an upright position. She felt the snag in the back of her tights start to run.

'Sofia?' he enquired, still with a gentle smile

'Yes. I am. Sofia, that is,' she stuttered, feeling herself blushing. 'I have an interview with Mr Williams?' she added, trying to rally her thoughts. The man laughed. 'I realised that. Come on, I'll take you up,' he replied, gesturing towards the elevators.

Feeling a desperate need to fill the void of silence that invaded the space as the doors slid shut, Sofia said, 'so how long have you worked for Sublime Retreats?'

'Oh, about ten years now,' he responded easily, 'I was originally a concierge for them on the island of Corfu in Greece but then… well, let's say my life changed, so I moved to Houston and started working at the offices here.'

Keen to glean any information she could before the meeting, she pressed on, 'So, what are they like to work for? And Mr Williams, is he a good boss?' she added conspiratorially, waggling her eyebrows to show that all secrets were safe with her.

He laughed, glancing sideways at her, a peculiar look on his face. 'It's a great company to work for. We're expanding at a good rate, yet keeping our standards high. That's why 'Mr Williams' needs a PA. And I believe he's a good boss.'

'That's good to hear,' she said, smoothing down the slightly too tight skirt of the suit she had bought for today. 'I'm nervous as hell.'

'No need to be nervous, he doesn't bite' the man answered as the doors swished open revealing an open plan workspace with floor to ceiling windows along the far wall, showing the incredible view that the building afforded. Momentarily awed, she stopped in her tracks, staring at the city skyline until the doors closed, bumping into her. She jumped forward, stumbling in her unfamiliar heels and dropping her bag. Feeling the eyes of the office on her, she hid behind the curtain of dark, glossy hair that fell forward as she scooped up the contents of her bag.

'Shit, I'm sorry,' she said, looking up into that grinning face. She couldn't believe she was making such a mess of things. Hopefully Mr Williams wasn't looking.

'Not to worry, come on,' he said, striding off towards the far end of the room to a door with a discreet plaque announcing it to be the office of Peter Williams. He opened the door, turned to her and said 'take a seat, would you like a coffee?'

'I'd love one, if I have time? Espresso, two sugars please.' Nodding, he left the room. She settled herself on the chair in front of a grand-looking desk, littered with piles of papers. If this was any indicator, then this Mr Williams needed help to get organised, she thought, idly wondering what he was going to be like. She imagined a grandfatherly type, who would take her under his wing and be grateful for her presence in his life, with her usual rose-tinted, Hallmark film-esque musings. The return of the man with the coffee disturbed from her daydream. He placed the small cup carefully on the desk in front of her. 'Thank you so much, I need this!' she said, taking a sip. 'By the way, I didn't catch your name?' she asked, looking up at him.

'My name is Mr Williams' he replied smoothly, taking his seat on the other side of the desk, pressing his tie into place with his hand, 'but you can call me Peter.' Horrified, she stared at him, mouth agape and muttered *'Che palle!'* under her breath before snapping it shut.

☼

Adam had glanced up briefly as Peter walked past with yet another potential P.A.. Shaking his head as he watched her spill the contents of her bag across the carpet, he quickly dismissed her from his mind as he got back to organising the upcoming trip to Italy. As Head of Product for the new 'City Breaks' program, he was working flat out to add to the portfolio. He had been the brainchild behind this new concept, and he was giving his all to make it work. Finding the perfect property, signing the contract, was his only desire right now. He was adamant that this trip was going to run smoothly. He had comprehensive plans for his career and his upward trajectory started with this project.

Sipping on his kale smoothie, he grimaced slightly as he continued responding to emails, checking and double checking timings along with locations. Trying to estimate how long it would take to get from one property to another in a city he had never been to before was tricky. He didn't want to make any mistakes. He had singled out Florence to launch the program after running a survey with the members of the club. As ever, Italy had come out as their imagined favourite European destination, and frankly Florence seemed to have the most to offer regarding dining out, sightseeing and tours, all things which were expected as standard by their clientele.

There were twenty potential properties he wanted to see; he was scheduling four appointments a day for the first five days. It was going to be tough going, but would leave them time to revisit the final contenders, and then single out the one apartment which would be the flagship for the entire program. It had to be perfect.

Deep in concentration, it seemed like only a short while later that Peter came back past with the girl. They were laughing together as they waited for the elevator; he took a moment to admire her shapely legs, eyes drawn by the ladder running the length of her left leg, before it arrived and carried her away. As Peter walked back Adam called out, 'No good, huh?' assuming the speed of the meeting showed a lack of interest.

Stopping by his desk, Peter smiled down in response. 'Quite the opposite, actually. She's fresh out of college, full of spark. I found her quite disarming. Most of the candidates I have seen so far have been way too full of themselves, it made a delightful change.'

'I'm not sure someone with no experience is the best idea, Peter' said Adam earnestly, pushing his glasses back into place, thinking of the precious upcoming trip and Peter's need for someone to look after things here while they were away. 'Have you got any more to see?' He knew that there were far more qualified people on the list. He had taken the time to check them out yesterday. Sofia Marino was probably the last one he would have picked, although her name seemed familiar, but he couldn't quite put his finger on why.

'Yes, I have another three interviews this afternoon,' Peter winced at the thought; he hated this entire process, 'so I shall hold off deciding until I see them all.' With a nod to Adam, he left him to carry on with his work.

Before he immersed himself back in the Italian schedule, Adam made a quick call to his dad. Since his mum had died seven years ago and his father had retired from the Police Force shortly after, a broken man, Adam had tried to involve himself in his life as much as possible, although the old fella didn't make it easy.

His Dad had always been a distant figure growing up, immersed in his work which he loved, his wife whom he adored even more, and seeming to have little regard for the small boy waiting to greet him after his shifts, giving him nothing more than a pat on the head as he made his way through the door. When his wife died, it was like it had knocked the stuffing out of him. The once powerful man shrinking in his uniform until it no longer fitted, hanging off him pathetically until the day he finally handed in his badge.

Now his life was comprised of card games with his buddies in the bar, along with a mild obsession with an old case that had never been solved, trying to prove the Mafia connection to a bank robbery that happened years ago. Jack's office in the family home was a testament to the case; the walls were plastered with photos, faded newspaper clippings - all reminiscent of any police drama ever seen on TV.

'Morning, Pop,' he said when the call was finally answered, 'how are you doing today?'

'Same old, same old, son. Just getting ready to go down to Murphy's, meeting the boys for an afternoon game. You should stop by on your way home.'

'I hope you've eaten something, dad?'

'Yes, yes. Of course I had a bite, and I can always grab a burger there later if it goes on a bit.'

Sighing at his father's complete disregard to healthy eating, Adam let it slide; they'd had that conversation too many times for him to fight it anymore. 'I might drop in after the gym. I'll see how late I am here. Otherwise I'll be over tomorrow to watch the game, ok?'

'Yup, looking forward to it, son, I've got some beers in, you bring some snacks.'

Ending the call, and forcing his dad out of his mind, Adam put his head down and got back to work. Before he knew it, it was 5pm and he could see his boss escorting the last of the candidates back to the elevators. Adam was packing up, getting ready to go to the fitness centre in the building, when Peter stopped by his desk, obviously on his way home.

'How's the trip shaping up?' his boss inquired.

'Pretty good, I think. Just waiting for the last few appointments to confirm, then we're all set. How about your hunt for the perfect P.A., do you think you've found the one?'

'Oh, I'm pretty sure I have found the right candidate. I will send an email out later to confirm. Don't train too hard!' Peter finished with a wave at Adam's gym bag, and ran to catch the lift that was just about to close on a group of rowdy colleagues, brimming with the Friday feeling, ready to wind down with a drink at their regular bar down the street.

When the elevator had expelled her out into the parking level after her interview, Sofia had let out the breath which she felt like she had been holding all the way down. It had seemed to go well. Luckily Peter was charming and didn't seem at all put out by her artless questions before the interview. Also, he loved cats. How bad could a person who loved cats be? As she wandered in the direction she had left her car, she hoped her father wouldn't give her the third degree about this morning, but resigned herself to the fact that he would. He couldn't help himself. She blamed his Sicilian blood for his dramatic responses to everything in life. She located her car, patting the hood lovingly before climbing in.

The 1972 Mercedes Benz Sl-Class 350 had been a gift from her uncle Joey when he moved back to Italy a few years ago. As impractical as it was, she loved everything about it. Even though her brothers teased her about it being a 'pimp's' car, especially with the leather upholstery, she refused to give it up and buy something more up to date. The engine purred to life as she turned the key and she carefully manoeuvred out of the tight parking space and drove down to the exit. When she finally merged onto the Gulf Freeway that would take her home, she turned on her radio and lowered the roof, enjoying the feel of the wind whipping her hair with the sun beating down on this late July afternoon.

Pulling up outside Margarita's, she waved at her youngest brother, Antonio, who was inside cleaning the windows. He brightened at the sight of her. Jumping off the chair he was standing on, he came to the door to greet her. Throwing the cloth he had been using onto a table before clutching her shoulders, he kissed her sloppily on both cheeks before asking, 'Well? How did it go?'

'Pretty good, we'll see. I should know by tomorrow morning.'

'Well, I think they will be lucky to have you, *Piccolo*'

'*Piccolo* was funny when I was five, not so much now I'm 25!'

He laughed, ruffling her hair 'you will always be *Piccolo* to me, sis, you know that' he turned, picking up the cloth he'd abandoned, as he climbed back up to finish the last of the windows. 'Ma and Pa are out back, you'd better go say hi' he grinned at her.

Taking a deep breath, she made her way through the main body of the restaurant, the familiar smells comforting as she readied herself for another argument with her father. She glanced back as she walked through, taking in the warm ochre tones of the walls, the highly polished leather seating booths and the small but functional bar of the restaurant that had been her home all her life, to take courage.

As she pushed through the swing doors that led to the kitchen she was greeted by a blast of heat, the heady, intoxicating smell of tomatoes steeped in garlic and basil, edged with the ever present hint of yeast as the pizza dough sat quietly proving in bowls on the counter. A wall of sound also greeted her. She had arrived in time for a full-blown Marino 'discussion' about possible changes to the menu. Her eldest brother Aldo looked up from his seat at the small desk in the far corner and shouted across to her. 'Sofia! Will you tell him that there is nothing wrong with trying something new?'

'*Magari*! I think it's a wonderful idea. We have had the same menu for forty years, a little change wouldn't hurt,' she replied laughing. She slipped off her jacket, hanging it on the brass rack on the wall before wandering over to the counter to pick at the cheese, cut up on the chopping board ready for tonight's service. She had a small smile on her face, thankful for this unexpected topic; winking at Aldo as they both mentally counted down for the explosion.

'Exactly!' her father erupted, his short, rotund frame vibrating with indignation. 'Why change it? Most of our customers have been coming here that long, and do you know why? Because they like the food! They have their favourite meals; they know every time they come here they will get exactly what they want.' He started pounding a pile of innocent chicken breasts into submission as an extension of his feeling about the matter.

Standing up, Aldo towered over his Father. The contrast was striking, made more amusing by the fact that he was the spitting image of him, just a good six inches taller.

'Papà, I understand what you are saying and I agree, up to a point' he added quickly, raising a hand to stop his father jumping in 'but, those people who have been coming here for forty years won't be coming in much longer. Not to put too fine a point on it, most of 'em will be buzzard bait soon enough'

'*Basta!*' scolded their mother, coming, unnoticed, back into the kitchen from the storeroom, causing them all to snap to attention and look at her. 'Aldo, I will not have you talking of death in here,' she chastised, pointing a finger accusingly at him 'and you!' she turned, aiming the finger at her husband who flinched under its force, 'will listen a little to your children. Yes, you are wise and experienced,' she continued as he preened under her praise, 'but they have new ideas, a fresh look on how the world is. Are you really so pig-headed that can't see things are changing around us? That our takings are dwindling away every year even though your *goombahs* come and hang out in here every day to talk themselves silly. Aldo, I suggest you get your ideas together with your brothers and sister; we can sit down tomorrow to talk them through. Sensibly.'

She glared at them all, daring anyone to disagree and, seeing no objections, beamed as if nothing had happened, her face lighting up instantly. '*Va bene*. I am going to Kroger's to get some supplies for tonight, Sofia, come with me.' With that, she stalked out the doors, leaving them swinging behind her. Meekly, Sofia retrieved her jacket from where she had hung it, following her mother out of the restaurant, keeping her head down and avoiding eye contact with her Father to prevent further conversation.

Outside, she found her Mother standing next to the Mercedes.

Squinting in the bright sunlight, Sofia slipped on her sunglasses and smiled at the wiry woman who could control the entire family with a well-pointed digit.

'You want me to drive, Mamma?' she called, reaching into her bag for her keys; she knew her mother would want to go in her car. Valentina had never admitted it, but her failing eyesight had caused her to bump her own car a few times recently. She seemed less and less inclined to drive herself, or go for an eye test for that matter.

'Yes please, Sofia, I need to add a few things to this list,' she responded airily, waving a piece of paper at her daughter before sliding into the passenger seat. They set off on the familiar route to Kroger's in easy silence, Valentina biting the end of her pen in between adding notes to her list. Eventually satisfied, she folded the paper, sliding it into the front pocket of her purse before placing it on the floor next to her feet.

'So, what's the deal, how'd it go today?' she asked her daughter suddenly, twisting a little in her seat to look at her. *'Papà* worried about you all morning.'

Surprised, Sofia cast a quick look at her Ma to see how serious she was, but saw no hint of jest in the woman's face. 'Really? Why would he worry?'

'You know, you might be as smart as a hooty owl, but you can be remarkably dense sometimes! Of course he is worried, if you don't get the job it will upset you, if you get it he feels like he is losing you, either way he will be unhappy.'

'Well butter my butt and call me a biscuit, I hadn't thought of it like that,' she declared. 'I thought he was just being contrary and well, you know, *Papà*. But I think it went well'

'Your father wants nothing but the best for you, Sofia, he has a hard time showing it is all. Just keep that in mind, however this goes.'

That evening, sitting with her five brothers, squashed into the booth in the restaurant where they always sat, she let the hubbub of banter, teasing and chatter wash over her, savouring the moment. She would really, really miss this if she got a place of her own. It was hard to imagine eating dinner by herself; she shied away from that thought as her mother arrived, plonked an enormous dish of Sofia's favourite Pasta Alla Norma on the table and demanded '*Mangia bene.*'

None of the six needed any encouragement and were soon ladling heaping portions of the tomato sauce laden rigatoni, studded with caramelised aubergine and laced with ricotta salata, onto their plates. The scent of garlic with basil erupted as they scooped up mouthfuls of the delicious meal, soaking up the remaining sauce with hunks of crusty bread their father had made that morning. Sofia grinned inwardly as she sipped on her wine. It was the only time she and her brothers were quiet, their love of wonderful food greater than their love of debate.

Only when the serving dish was empty, wiped almost clean by Aldo, did the conversation start up again. The question of new ideas for the menu sparking a lively conversation among her brothers. Sofia knew from experience she had to let this run its course before adding her own thoughts, so she collected the empty plates laden with cutlery and took them through to the kitchen.

Her Mother nodded her approval at the almost spotless dishes as Sofia placed them in the sink where she was washing up. Wiping away an errant strand of dark hair with the back of her arm she said, 'there's some Cannoli over there,' she gestured in the dessert's direction with her chin, 'it's ricotta with dark chocolate today!'

'Mamma, are you deliberately making all my favourite foods?' Sofia enquired.

'I don't know what you mean, little one,' her Mother replied innocently, studiously scrubbing a pan. Walking up behind her, leaning in, she wrapped her hands around her tiny waist, squeezing her affectionately.

'I will always want to come home wherever I go,' she whispered 'whether or not you cook.'

Valentina placed the pan carefully back into the soapy water, pulled off her rubber gloves, and turned to embrace her daughter.

'Your Father is not the only one who finds your desire to fly from the nest difficult, you know? You are my baby and my daughter. I know I will lose you one day to a husband. This is the beginning of that journey.'

Laughing through the tears that had sprung up, Sofia stood back a little to look her mother in the face, the one that was so similar to her own. 'You won't get rid of me that easily' she grinned. 'I am trying to find a job, not a man, you know that's the last thing on my list of priorities!' she chortled. 'And can you imagine a man who can face my brothers?' They both exploded with laughter at the very thought. God forbid a man would pay attention to *Piccolo*. There would be hell to pay!

Giving her Ma one last squeeze, she grabbed the platter of Cannoli, salivating at the mere sight of it. She carried it easily through to the restaurant, hitting the swing doors with her hip with practiced ease to let her walk through.

LA BOCCA DI BOTERO

(Botero's mouth)

From: Peterwilliams@sublimeretreats.com

To: sofiamarino@yahoo.com

Subject: Contract

Dear Sofia,

I am delighted to confirm your position with us as my Personal Assistant. I have attached your contract, have a read through and if you are happy with the terms please sign and return.

Assuming all is well, I look forward to seeing you on Monday morning. If you can come in for 8am, we will have a chance to sit and discuss what I need from you in this role, before the usual workday starts at nine.

I look forward to hearing from you.

Best regards,

Peter

Peter Williams

General Manager–*Sublime Retreats*

Adam was pulling up outside his parents' house, he still thought of it that way, in Pasadena, when the email came through from Peter announcing that Sofia Marino would be his new Personal Assistant. Eyebrows lifted in surprise at the choice. He thought of the ramifications if she wasn't up to the job as he popped the trunk to retrieve the groceries he'd bought on his way here.

He and his dad shared little in common except their love of baseball and their support of the Astros, although Jack still insisted on calling them the Colt's. They had a standing date to watch the weekend games. Whatever was happening in their lives, it was their one constant.

'Hi Pop, it's me,' he called as he let himself in, awkwardly juggling the bags of shopping as he turned his key, then making his way to the kitchen down the hall to unpack the groceries. As usual, he tried to ignore the happy family photos that lined the walls, but he couldn't avoid the familiar, memory laden scent of home.

'Pop?' he called again, a little louder, when there was no response.

'I'm in here, son,' came the reply. Adam grinned, knowing exactly where he would find him. Walking through the lounge to the study on the far side, he pushed the door open to see his father sat at his desk, elbow deep in photographs and newspaper cuttings.

'Find anything new?' he asked, out of habit rather than expectation.

'There's something I'm missing. I can feel it. It's like when you have a word on the tip of your tongue–this is on the tip of my brain. It's so damn frustrating!'

'Well, it's nearly game time. How 'bout you finish up and we have a beer?'

'You go ahead Son; I'll be there in a minute.'

Shaking his head, but leaving him to it, Adam went back to the kitchen, grabbing a cold beer from the fridge. He worried about the old man's obsession sometimes, but he worried more about what he would do if he ever cracked the case. It seemed to be the one thing that kept him going. He popped the top off the bottle, took a swig, then put it on the counter as he prepared game snacks.

Every time it was his turn to provide the nibbles, he attempted to make it as healthy as possible. He shuddered every time he opened his dad's fridge, the piles of ready meals alongside high-fat snacks laying testament to the old man's complete disregard of every piece of information Adam had supplied him with. His father did not seem to care one jot about his health and constantly told him to butt out, declaring that he would rather live a few years enjoying himself than many years eating rabbit food.

He set about cutting up some cucumber, brilliant red peppers and carrots into sticks for the humus and guacamole he had bought. He put a pan of water on to boil to make some hard-boiled eggs before preparing a platter, adding mixed salad leaves as a base, building up from there with the selection of low fat meats and cheeses he had bought. Artfully arranging everything to look as enticing as possible, he stood back to admire his work as his dad came into the kitchen.
Jack looked at the food, his face impassive. Turning to open the cupboard above the work surface, he pulled out an enormous bag of Doritos. He silently opened another cupboard, grabbed a large bowl, and tipped the entire bag into it. He looked at Adam, waiting to see if he had something to say.

Adam ignored the old mans' contrariness and just picked up the platter in his right hand, grasping his beer in his left. 'Are we all set?' he asked and when his dad replied, 'sure' walking through to the lounge, Adam followed to take up their familiar positions. As usual, their conversation revolved mainly around gameplay for most of the next couple of hours. It was only during a break between innings that his dad asked about his life and how work was going.

Adam told him about his excitement for his upcoming trip, trying not to bore him too much with the details, but making him understand the importance of it, how thrilling it was to be travelling to Europe. Never having left the states before, he was actually quite nervous about it. He'd flown many times across the US, but this was going to be something else.

'Well son, it sounds like you've got things pretty sewn up as far as organising it goes, don't seem like anything could go wrong.'

'We'll see. Peter has just employed a new PA and I'm really not sure she will be up to holding the fort whilst he's away.' He took a thoughtful swig of beer 'I really don't understand why he picked Sofia Marino when there were so many others to choose from. It doesn't make sense.'

Jack had paused, beer halfway to his mouth. He turned to look at Adam, although the next innings had started. 'What did you say her name was?'

'Sofia Marino, why?'

'I'll tell you why son, hang on a minute' he jumped up and went quickly through to his office, returning moments later with a faded newspaper clipping, removing the pin that had held it on the wall for so long as he strode back into the room. He handed it silently to Adam, who took in the headline and felt things fall into place.

'Marino acquitted of bank robbery' the headline screamed, followed by the scathing account of bungled police work and mysterious retractions of statements which led to the man being released. Of course! No wonder that name had sounded familiar, he'd been looking at it for so many years he didn't see it anymore, but it had obviously lodged in his brain.

'They never worked out who his accomplice was,' his Pa said as Adam was reading about the elusive second masked gunman. All anybody involved in the heist could say with any conviction was that he was shorter than Marino, slender, never spoke a word - leading the police to believe they had flown him in for the job and possibly did not speak English.

Jack picked up his beer and waved it in his direction. 'If she is part of that family, then that'll be why she got the job. Your boss probably didn't have any choice in the matter! Do you know anything else about her?'

'No, not really,' said Adam thoughtfully, 'but I intend to find out…'

☼

Sofia arrived at the office a good half an hour before she was due to meet Peter. Her nerves had woken her up early, so she had showered and got dressed before making her way down to the kitchen. Giovanni was already there, sat on a stool gazing out of the window. She could smell the coffee. She smiled, 'good morning, *Papà*,' she called quietly so as not to startle him. He looked up and beamed at her.

'*Buongiorno, Piccolo*, I have prepared some coffee for you.'

'Thanks *Papà*, I need it today. I didn't really sleep that well, I'm tuckered out before I begin!'

She sat down on the stool next to his as he pulled forward a demitasse cup, gently poured in the coffee and added two sugars, just as she liked it. He stirred it carefully so as not to slop it over the rim of the tiny cup, and once he was satisfied, he slid it over to her. Taking her first, grateful sip, she gave her thanks then said, 'what's got you up so early? I wasn't expecting to see anyone this morning.'

'I wanted to wish you good luck on your first day, sweetheart,' he replied, his gaze now focused on her. Sofia was taken aback. He had been decidedly quiet since she had announced that she had got the position. Despite what her mother had said, she really did not think he approved and probably never would.

'That means a lot to me *Papà*; I honestly didn't think you were happy about this.'

'Happy about losing my only daughter to the big city? No. But proud of my only daughter for striking out, doing what she believes she should do? Yes.'

Stunned, she felt tears prick her eyes and trying not to rub them lest she smudge her mascara; she sniffed, stood, and hugged him.

'Thank you. That means an awful lot to me, *Papà*. I will try to continue to make you proud.' She mumbled into his neck. Pulling away, she saw he was bright eyed too, they shared a tender look.

'Anyway, here, I have made you some lunch to take with you,' he said brusquely, 'who knows what the restaurants are like around there! '

Laughing, she took the proffered bag, and feeling a little more confident that she could face the day ahead, drained her coffee and with a last smile of thanks set out for the big, wicked city.

She was sitting in her car, still marvelling at her father's behaviour this morning, when Peter pulled in beside her. He gave her a cheery wave, and they both got out of their cars.

'Good Morning Sofia. Glad to see you are punctual!' he called as he bent to retrieve his briefcase from the backseat. Still impressed by his English accent, she looked at him shyly, saying, 'I wasn't sure how long it would take this time of day so...' she trailed off.

'How long have you been sitting there?' he asked knowingly.

She laughed and admitted, 'a good half an hour!'

'In that case, I think our first job this morning is to get you some coffee,' he chuckled, gesturing towards the elevators. Relaxing a little, Sofia followed him and soon they arrived on the floor for the office. Her office! She could hardly believe she was there and she would now be part of this amazing company. Trying to contain her excitement, she followed Peter through to the kitchen.

☼

She and Peter were ensconced in his office, heads together, in deep conversation when Adam arrived. He'd come in early hoping to grab another look at her application form to see what else was on there, but with them already here it was impossible.

He hung his jacket over the back of his chair and started up his Mac before walking down the carpeted length of the office to the kitchen to put his carefully prepared salad in the fridge and pick up a glass of water. As he walked back, Peter looked up, calling him in to his office.

'Good Morning Adam, I'd like you to meet Sofia, my new assistant,' Peter said as Adam entered the room. Forcing a delighted look onto his face, Adam looked at the girl that was causing him so much worry, taken aback at how pretty she was. He hadn't seen her clearly when she came in for the interview, but as she stood to shake hands with him, her face lit up with a smile that was quite beatific. He felt a bolt of electricity shoot through him as their hands met that left his stomach fizzing and his lower regions stirring. Startled by his body's reaction, he desperately tried to cover it, briefly shaking her hand before dropping it, giving her a curt nod.

'Welcome to the team, Sofia,' he said, his dour face and small grimace reminiscent of a Botero painting, belying the sentiment.

Dropping back into her seat, Sofia was confused. She felt sure that an actual spark had flown between them when their hands had touched; equally sure he felt it too; she had seen the shock register in his beautiful blue eyes. But he was looking at her now like he disliked her intensely, which was insane, they'd only just meet. She lowered her eyes, desperately trying to think of something to say.

Peter, sensing something amiss but unable to fathom what it could be, said, 'I will hold a meeting later so I can formally introduce Sofia to everybody, but it's good that you two get to meet now. You are going to working closely together these next few weeks before Adam and I leave for Florence Sofia. Adam is coordinating the entire trip so you can field questions he has about arrangements on my behalf.'

Sofia's face lit up again 'Oh Florence, that's amazing. I would love to go there!' she exclaimed. 'The Duomo, Ponte Vecchio, the museums, the galleries, I dream of visiting the Uffizi. Wow, you are going to have an amazing time,' she carried on. Hearing herself gushing, she snapped her mouth shut, not confident yet to expand on her love of art and culture with these well-travelled people.

'Well, it will be just Peter and I,' Adam said churlishly. 'You, apparently, will hold the fort while we are away.' With another brief, close mouthed smile, he turned and walked out the door and back to his desk.

'Is he always that cheerful?' Sofia asked, wondering what made a gorgeous man like that so grumpy.

'Looking up from his computer screen, Peter frowned slightly and replied, 'not usually, maybe just a bad morning. Don't take it personally.' He winked reassuringly at her 'you can meet the rest of the team in a bit, but for now let's go over my schedule for the upcoming week.'

At his desk, Adam was chewing the inside of his cheek in consternation. He'd made a complete ass of himself with that girl in front of Peter; hopefully his boss hadn't paid too much attention to his reaction. Deciding he had nothing to gain from obsessing over her and her family connections, he absorbed himself in work. Final plans for Florence in place, he was already looking ahead to where he could extend the City Breaks program next. San Sebastian in Spain had caught his attention. A vibrant city with beaches sounded perfect. He was putting out feelers to find reputable property agents there.

A message popped through on the company's intranet system announcing a meeting at 10am. He scowled at it. He didn't particularly want to waste more time 'meeting' Sofia, but he guessed he ought to make up for this morning's debacle. Shortly before ten he traipsed through to the large, airy meeting room where the rest of the staff were assembling in dribs and drabs, chattering amongst themselves. He caught snippets of conversation of the 'what I did at the weekend' variety as he went to sit near the front, to make sure Peter was aware he had shown up.

A few minutes later Peter strode in, trailed by a nervous-looking Sofia who was glancing around but not focusing on any point in particular and as she stood next to Peter at the front, positioned herself slightly behind him, twisting the rings on her fingers as if her life depended upon it. Adam felt a little sorry for her. He couldn't help but think that maybe he and his dad had jumped the gun a little on thinking she was part of some big crime family.

'Good morning, everyone.' Peter's cool British tones rang out, calling everyone to attention. 'Thank you for joining me today. I have a few things to discuss with you before we crack on with our week!'

First off, I would like to introduce the newest member of our team,' he glanced to one side, then looked further behind to find her, gently reaching out and touching her arm to encourage her forward. 'This is Sofia, my assistant, who has started with us today. She's going to have a busy couple of weeks getting to grips with everything before Adam and I leave for Europe, so please, everyone be kind, and if you see her wandering in the hallway looking lost, please point her toward my office!'

There was a ripple of laughter at this; even Sofia found the grace to grin. Along with the cries of 'Welcome on board' there was a smattering of applause, which soon petered away as their MD continued. He laid out this month's targets, and the proposed advertising campaign that was in place to launch City Breaks; Peter kept the meeting short but imparted the information and encouragement they needed adeptly. One of his many leadership skills was the ability not to bore the pants off people in these necessary weekly round ups, they all loved him for that.

When the meeting finished, Adam pushed his way through the milling stragglers, trying to catch up with Sofia before she became entrenched in Peter's office again. He had decided to make an effort to get to know the girl, let's face it; if he had to go through her to get to the boss, it would be worth putting in some groundwork now to build a good relationship. At least's that what he was telling himself as he trotted to catch up with her, picking up speed as he saw her reaching the doorway.

'Sofia,' he called out as her hand touched the door of the office, 'hold up, I wanted to ask you something.' He jogged the last few steps and plastered a grin on his face, 'look, about this morning. I was a bit rude I think.'

She arched an eyebrow at him, a small smirk playing delightfully around her lips, but didn't say a word.

'So I thought maybe I could take you for lunch?' he surprised himself by asking, under her chocolate-brown eyed stare 'um, you know, if you'd like to that is?'

She paused for a moment, seeming to enjoy his discomfort, before replying, 'Sure. I think that would be swell. My Pa gave me some food for today but I reckon' it'll keep,' then she unleashed that smile again which made his knees give way imperceptibly. 'I think Peter is aiming for us to take a break about one if that suits?'

Nodding, finding words scarce, but social norms came into play and he distantly heard himself say 'I'll meet you in the lobby at one then,' before swivelling on the spot and making a break for his desk. He found he was panting when he reached his chair, like he'd just done a complete workout, not ask a colleague out for lunch. It was most alarming. He took a long drink of water to settle his thoughts before hitting a key to wake up his computer and sat, thoughtfully polishing his glasses.

Still standing by the door, Sofia was feeling equally discombobulated. She had been sure that Adam didn't like her, but here he was getting all tongue tied just asking her for a work lunch; she was sure that's all it was; it was all very confusing. But she was happy to take the olive branch, she had a feeling she needed to get on well with this man, from what she had learnt so far, he played a big role in the company, Peter relied on him a lot, so it made sense that they should have a good relationship.

What better way to start that off than over lunch? As her Mother was fond of saying '*A tavola non si invecchi*a', you don't get old at the table, and she was thrilled to be going out to eat at a restaurant that wasn't Margarita's, she couldn't remember the last time that had happened.

One O'clock found her engulfed in the chair in the lobby again as she waited for Adam to appear. She was sending an SMS to her friend Suzie to see if she was free to meet up tonight. What with one thing and another, they hadn't seen each other for over a week. It was high time they corrected that. It delighted her when Suzie responded immediately with her trademark string of emoji's, which seemed to imply that she was up for it. She saw Adam emerge from the elevator, so she quickly tapped away a message to say that she would swing by at 7pm to pick her up, before locking her phone and slipping into the pocket of her bag.

She stood up, unaided this time, smiling as he approached; he faltered a moment, but then found his step again, crossing the expanse of the lobby quickly.

'Hi, glad you could get away. Where do you fancy eating?'

'I don't know this area so well. What do you recommend?' she asked, genuinely interested in what was available and where he liked to go.

'There's a place just a few blocks down that does great salads, sandwiches and burgers, depending what you're in the mood for?'

'Sounds perfect. I didn't have breakfast this morning. I am starving now!' she laughed and followed him through the doors onto the busy sidewalk.

It was a brilliantly sunny day again; it felt warm outside after the air-conditioned offices so they both discarded their jackets, Sofia folding hers neatly over one arm, Adam casually hooking his on a finger and throwing it over his shoulder.

'So how have you found things so far?' he asked, looking down at her. She really was quite petite. Glancing quickly up at him before having to sidestep around dithering pedestrians, she replied, 'I am a little overwhelmed to be honest, there's so much to remember.' He nodded. He remembered his first few weeks with the company, how terrified he had been of making a mistake. The members of the club paid huge fees to join, and that was before they even travelled anywhere. It wasn't an environment where mistakes were tolerated.

He led her into a restaurant simply called Local Foods, the busy atmosphere backed his recommendation, it was obviously a very popular lunch spot. Sofia took in the airy space, brightened with light wood, vibrant turquoise booths and benches as they grabbed a seat at a table along the wall. A waiter quickly came by with a pitcher of water and menus. Adam swiftly picked his favourite Asian chicken salad with a glass of orange juice. Sofia seemed to be torn, and took a while before ordering the 44 Farms Burger with homemade fries and roasted corn succotash on the side, accompanied by a large glass of coke.

'You weren't kidding when you said you were hungry,' he laughed, unable to believe this tiny girl was going to park away all that food. But park it away she did. He watched in amazement as she chatted away easily to him, in between enormous bites of her meal and groans of appreciation of the food. He had never seen anybody devour anything with such relish. It captivated him, barely eating his own lunch, pushing the salad around his plate in a vague approximation of eating.

When she finally put her cutlery down, wiping her mouth rather daintily for one who had just gorged on a feast fit for a quarterback, she leaned back, rubbing her belly with the contended air of a cat.

'That was damn fine fixin's,' she stated, 'who knew café food could be so good… that gives me an idea' her eyes stared off into the distance as she inspected her plan. 'Hmm,' she added to nobody in particular.

'Earth to Sofia,' Adam called after a few moments of waiting expectantly for her to re-join him. 'What's going on in that head of yours?' he laughed as he signalled to the server for the check.

'Oh, it's just my family were having a big argument about the menu at our restaurant,' she smiled at some inside joke as she thought of them, 'my brothers want to upgrade the menu, add some modern dishes but my *Papà* won't hear of it but I have just had an idea that may solve the problem! Here let me…'

He waived away her attempt at paying her share of the bill, standing to one side as she pulled herself out from her seat by the wall, picking up her bag and her coat.

'So your family has a restaurant?'

'Yeah, big surprise, huh? The Italian family with a restaurant,' she grinned disarmingly as they made their way back out to the street.

'So, where is this place? I might have been there.'

'Oh I doubt it, unless you head out to Galveston Wall much?'

Adam stopped dead in his tracks, turning to look at her, causing busy passers-by to tut loudly at the obstruction. 'Galveston? As in the Balinese Room? Famous for supposedly inventing the Margarita?'

'One and the same, that's what our restaurant is called, Margarita's. My dad kinda had a thing for that era, his dad used to work at the Balinese Room in its heyday. The stories he could tell. He met Frank Sinatra!'

And she was off again, chattering away. The sounds of her words wafting over his head as Adam's brain scrambled to remember everything his father had ever told him about that big Mafia family and their hold on the area known as Galveston. By the time they arrived back at the entrance to the office, his brain was whirling. He startled when Sofia suddenly squealed and ran to hug a huge, broad shouldered, well-dressed man who was loitering by the door who walked forward to meet her.

'Aldo, what are you doing here? And looking so smart?' she cried, standing back a little to admire him in his business suit 'what's this all about?' She'd only ever seen him dressed up like this for funerals, even then he complained about it, much preferring his jeans and t-shirts as a rule.

'I'll tell you later *Piccolo*, but I just wanted to stop by to see how you were doing.'

'So far so good,' she responded happily, 'everyone has been great. In fact, Adam just took me for lunch.' She looked around until she saw him, skulking near the door, unsure what to do, trying not to draw attention to himself. 'Adam,' she called, 'come over here' and he tried to look enthusiastic as he made his way over to where the man was now leaning nonchalantly against the wall.

'Adam, this Aldo, my eldest brother,' she gushed. The two men eyed each other warily. Adam stretched out a hand; 'pleased to meet you,' he said into the stern face, preparing himself for what he knew was to come. The iron like grip brought tears to his eyes and he could feel metacarpals' crunching together as his hand was given a short, sharp jerk before being released. Aldo leaned forward, 'pleased to meet you Mr Adam, I hope you are taking care of our Sofia?' he growled in a way that sent a primordial shiver up Adam's spine.

'Yes, yes, I think Sofia is a significant addition to our team,' Adam mumbled, 'but I must get back to work now. Come up whenever you like Sofia,' he said as scuttled through the doors to safety as fast as he could. Aldo resumed lounging against the wall, a smirk on his handsome face.

'What is wrong with you!' demanded Sofia 'that poor man just took me to lunch as a gesture of goodwill and welcome, then you have to terrify him, honestly Aldo,' she scolded.

'Believe me when I say no man taking you for lunch is doing it out of the goodness of his heart, little one. I am just looking out for you, that's all. You're too trusting.'

Sighing exasperatedly, she glanced at the time. 'Look, I'd better get back to work. Are we still on for the big family meeting later? I've had a great idea!'

'Yes, it's still on, I have a few ideas of my own,' he added mysteriously before giving her a hug 'look out for yourself *Piccolo*, I will see you later.' He planted a kiss on top of her head before striding off down the street, attracting covetous looks from the women he passed.

L'AMORE È CIECO

(Love is blind)

The rest of the afternoon disappeared in a haze of introductions, a notebook full of login details for all the new systems she had to get to grips with, along with far too much coffee. When Sofia finally got back in her car, she let out a groan and sat there quietly for five minutes before starting the engine and her journey home. Her brain was racing for the entire drive, she barely noticed her route. So much information to absorb had fried her senses. She couldn't help but worry if she was up to the task ahead. She had tried to track down Adam before she left, to thank him again for lunch, but he'd been remarkably absent every time she went to his desk, which was very odd. Never mind, she could catch up with him tomorrow.

She pulled up outside the restaurant with relief, looking forward to pulling on something more comfortable and then eating a large portion of whatever her mother had made for dinner. She had completely forgotten about the family meeting but was quickly reminded as she walked into a cacophony of noise as several members of the Marino family tried to make themselves heard. Sighing, she pulled off her jacket, placed her bag on the floor, and slid into the seat next to Antonio.

He placed his hand on her arm on the table by way of greeting but kept his eyes glued to the main event. Aldo was pacing up and down, unable to contain his frustration. Her Father, perched on a barstool, looked obstinate and implacable.

'Papa,' Aldo moaned, 'what is the point of having this meeting if you are going to shoot down every suggestion we make?'

'If you made sensible suggestions, we would not have this problem,' his father retorted.

Valentina interjected, 'Boys, I think it is time for a drink,' and pushed herself out of her seat with obvious effort.

'I want nothing,' said Giovanni truculently, causing her head to snap in his direction.

'You might not, but I definitely do!' she said and stomped through to the kitchen.

Sofia used the moment of silence to jump into the fray. 'OK, do you want to bring me up to speed, what have I missed?'

The two main protagonists maintained a grim, sulky silence, so Antonio filled the void.

'Basically, we have come up with a selection of ideas for Specials for the menu to try out, as well as theme nights, Aldo thinks it would be good to focus on the cuisine of different regions of Italy, and we agree,' he looked to their other brothers for support. The twins Luca and Flavio nodded their heads enthusiastically at Sofia, Roberto piping up 'we all believe this would be a good way forward but Papa will not listen to any of it.'

Sofia looked at her Father who had the air of a naughty schoolboy. 'Papa, why are you not at least thinking about any of this? You know we need to do something...' she said meaningfully. Since she had finished college she had been in charge of the books. She knew full well that they were struggling. Her parents had made her promise not to say anything to her brothers, but it was becoming harder to keep that secret. He looked up at her quickly, shaking his head to remind her of her promise.

Aldo took this motion to mean he was refusing yet again to contemplate their ideas and, hands gesticulating wildly, exploded 'Basta! Enough of this nonsense. If you don't have the sense to move forward with the times, then we will have to move forward by ourselves.'

'What's that supposed to mean?' Giovanni asked peevishly, fiddling with a napkin on the bar top.

'It means, Papa, that I had a meeting with the bank today. They have agreed to loan my brothers and me enough money that we can start our own restaurant.'

There was an exclamation of 'Dio mio!' followed by an almighty crash as Valentina dropped the tray holding the carafe of family wine and enough glasses for them all. Sofia leapt up to help, grabbing the broom and mop next to the door, thrusting them at Aldo before leading her mother gently to a seat.

'What blasphemy is this?' Valentina whispered, looking sternly from one boy to another until each hung his head in shame. 'This,' she exclaimed proudly, stabbing at the air with her finger, 'is a *family* restaurant and it will stay that way, do you hear?'

Sofia glanced at Aldo, who was industriously clearing up the mess, surprised at his bravery and, frankly, his business acumen. He must have put forward a compelling proposal to justify a loan. She then looked at her Father who was ashen; the news had obviously shocked him to the core.

'Antonio, go get some more drinks. I think we could all use one right now,' she ordered, and her brother scuttled off obediently, glad to be out of the war zone.

'Right, you two,' she announced, pulling Aldo's attention away from the spillage, her father's away from his internal turmoil. 'I think I have an idea where you can both get want you want.'

They all looked at her then; she flinched a little at being the centre of attention and was glad of Antonio's return. As he placed glasses in front of each of them, then studiously poured the wine, she continued, 'it occurred to me today that we can improve our profits and allow the boys to experiment a little without having all this drama.'

She reached down, picking up her glass, taking a healthy slug before carrying on. 'At the moment, we only open in the evenings. I realised today that we are missing out on a whole other market of clientele, the lunchtime crowd.' She stopped to allow this to sink in. She saw a slow smile of understanding appear on her Mother's face, Valentina always being one step ahead of the men in the family.

'What are you talking about, girl?' her father demanded.

'I am talking about opening up during the day, with a completely different menu to attract a completely different crowd. Aldo and the boys have come up with some fantastic ideas by the sounds of it, it would be foolish for…' she paused, then settled on '*us* to ignore them and we should at least try them out.'

She plonked herself back down on her seat, exhausted now, and watched the various members of her family absorb her idea. Aldo was beaming, his mind already racing ahead; it would seem, with putting his ideas into practice. Her Father was nodding his head ever so slightly as he turned the plan over, realising that he could still have things his way in the evenings. Finally, her gaze landed on Valentina, who gave her a sly wink and raised her glass in salute. Sofia grinned, raising hers in response; it seemed the battle was won, if not the war.

Sofia excused herself, leaving her family happily discussing the alternative plans for the restaurant, and made her way wearily up to her bedroom. Slipping off her shoes, she sighed in relief as her feet hit the carpet; she unzipped her skirt, letting it slide to the floor. Quickly discarding the rest of her clothes, she walked towards the bathroom, stopped, walked back, and picked everything up. She hung her suit neatly in the wardrobe, discarding what remained in the laundry basket. As keen as she was to shower and get ready to meet Suzie, she knew she would have to wear the suit again tomorrow; it was the only one she had for now.

After a reviving shower, she pulled on her jeans and a t-shirt before sitting at her dressing table to flick on some mascara. Her eyes landed on her tattered violin case, abandoned on the dresser, untouched for at least a month now. She had been so busy. There was a pang of guilt as she looked at the posters around her room. Classical musicians like Fabio Biondi fighting for space with more modern players such as Davide Rossi.

She could remember when Uncle Joey had presented her with her first violin. She must have been about five. It had nearly been as big as her. But the gentle, patient man had taken the time to show her how to coax beautiful sounds from it, and she had been hooked ever since. There had been a period in her teens, after seeing a Vanessa-Mae concert, when she dreamed of becoming a famous player, but as her interest in boys and then a career encroached, her lessons slipped, eventually fading away. Now she satisfied herself with playing for the pure love of it and at the occasional family function.

Running a brush through her dark, still damp hair, she tousled it slightly with her fingers before standing up, collecting her bag and making her way back downstairs. It relieved her to see her Father and Aldo in deep discussion at the table where she had left them, Aldo furiously scribbling notes on a pad. Her Mother, cleaning glasses behind the bar, smiled as she walked in.

'Well, Piccolo, you seem to have shown them the way,' she said with a nod in the table's direction. 'I am sorry this nonsense distracted from your first day. How was it?'

'It was exciting and exhausting, Mama,' Sofia replied, perching on a stool by the bar, 'but I think I am going to like it there. Are you OK? You look a little pale.'

'I am a bit tired, but don't worry. I shall have a lie down once I have finished with these,' she said, holding up a wine glass.

'Do you want me to do that?' she asked, looking at her mother with concern.

'Off with you, child!' said Valentina, flapping the cloth at her.

Sofia grinned at her Mother 'If you're sure? I am going to meet Suzie for a well-deserved drink!'

Laughing, Valentina said, 'Good for you. Send Suzie my love; tell her to come over soon. I haven't fed her for ages; I bet she's not eating properly!' Assuring her she would pass the message on, Sofia walked happily out, unnoticed by the men so deeply engrossed in their discussion.

Suzie flung the door of her apartment in response to Sofia's knock with a shout of 'Babe!' and a bear hug that lifted her off her feet. Laughing as she broke free, Sofia said 'anyone would think we haven't seen each other for a year!' She took the proffered glass from her friend and, sniffing it carefully, looked up inquiringly, 'what's in this, Suzie?'

'It's a new cocktail I have invented to celebrate your new job, it's called the Sublime,' she answered with a grin 'drink up!'

As ever, unable to resist that mischievous look and challenge to embrace life that had been leading her into trouble since she was five, Sofia took a slug from the potent brew, happy to discover it didn't taste too bad.

Pulling her by her sleeve further into the room, Suzie called over her shoulder, 'come on, sit and tell me all about your day while I finish getting ready.'

Sofia obediently followed her through the small but orderly lounge to the bedroom, which was showing all the signs of one of Suzie's indecisive clothes frenzies. The room was strewn with discarded outfits, so Sofia used her free hand to pluck a couple from the floor before dumping them on the bed, and sat on the stool by the window, sipping her drink while Suzie seated herself in front of the mirror to finish her makeup.

'So how was your first day in the dream job?' she asked as she deftly applied eyeliner in a way Sofia could only dream of. 'Was it like the first day of high school or slightly less terrifying?'

Thinking back to their first day together at Ball High, Sofia smiled. Yes, it had been terrifying, but at least they had had each other for moral support. 'Not so bad, although I was nervous as a fly in the glue pot.' She laughed, 'no mean girls so far, and I haven't worked out who the cool kids are yet!'

'Ah, hopefully, they will let you join their gang,' Suzie replied, picking up her Sublime and taking a sip. 'How about a crush? Every office has a heartthrob; there must be a hunk that's caught your eye?'

Sofia felt herself blushing as she flashed back to that electric moment when she and Adam had shook hands. Aware that Suzie was staring at her in the mirror, she shook her head quickly, saying, 'oh, not yet.'

'Sofia Marino, don't lie to me! I can tell by your face there was someone!'

Knowing better than trying to bluff someone who knew her better than she knew herself, Sofia admitted, 'well, there is this guy, Adam. I'm sure we had a moment when we met. He even took me to lunch, which was wonderful.'

'But?'

'But he seemed to avoid me for the rest of the day. It was weird, I wanted to thank him for lunch but he was nowhere to be found.'

Draining the last of her drink thoughtfully, Suzie asked, 'did something happen at lunch? Did you do something weird to put him off, like eat half a cow like you usually do or talk the legs off his chair?'

Grinning, Sofia said, 'I think it's safe to say I did both those things, but it didn't seem to bother him at all.'

'Must have been something else then, or maybe nothing.'

'Mighta been the fact that Aldo stopped by to say howdy,' Sofia said casually, well aware of her friend's feelings about her big brother. It was Suzie's turn to blush, her fair skin making it even more evident, but she laughed.

'That'd do it, honey. Poor boy, for God's sake, don't tell him yet there's another four like him back home! What the heck was Aldo doing in town?'

'He was getting a bank loan, would ya believe? He is so sick of Pa not letting him have any control at Margarita's that he was planning to up sticks, get his own place, taking the other fools with him.'

Suzie choked back a snort; she could just imagine how that idea would go down.

'But I think I've settled things, told them to open up at lunchtimes, let him have free rein then to try out his fancy ideas.'

'You see, that's what I love about you,' said her friend, getting up to pull a jacket out of the wardrobe 'brains as well as beauty.'

'By the way, Ma says to come and let her feed you,' Sofia replied quickly to cover up her discomfort at the compliment and getting up. 'She always thinks you're gonna starve to death.'

They both laughed, Suzie's willowy frame had always been a source of concern for Valentina. 'Come on girl; let's go get us a drink!' Suzie said, picking up her keys from the bowl on the table by the front door before leading the way outside.

The next week passed in a blur for Sofia. Sucked into her work environment by increments, absorbing facts, and understanding the workings of the company and her role within it daily. It left little room in her head for anything else. Relief flooded her when the weekend finally came, and she could relax a little.

She was vaguely aware of the plans back at the restaurant for the grand lunchtime opening the following Saturday, but beyond that, she had left them to it. Apart from the occasional flair up, Aldo and her pa seemed to be rubbing along nicely; there was a sense of excitement about the place as the rest of the family chipped in with ideas.

She even found time on Sunday to pick up her violin, spending a wonderful, absorbing hour reacquainting herself with the music she loved so much. She realized Aldo was standing in the doorway of her bedroom as she played the last notes of Chaconne, her favourite Bach piece. Its melancholy notes absorbed her but left her feeling uplifted. It took the slow clapping from her brother to bring her back to the present.

'Brava, Piccolo, that was amazing,' he said, his look of wonder emphasising his heartfelt words.

'Thanks, Bro; it's been a while since I've played. I'm a little rusty,' she said as she placed her beloved instrument back in its case, much in the manner of a mother putting her sleeping babe to bed. He smiled lovingly at her, 'well it didn't sound like it. Ma said to come get you for lunch.'

'Excellent! I'm starving,' she announced, clicking the case shut, and went with him down to the restaurant. The other men of the family were already seated, so she slid into her regular seat next to Antonio. There was the usual excited chatter and ribbing from her brothers, which was silenced only by Valentina's arrival, bearing a steaming plate of Pasta con le sarde which they all gazed at in rapture as she placed it on the table. As the smell of the fennel reached her nose, Sofia heard her mother say, 'Sofia, please go get the salad, and bring some more wine while you are there,' she added, eyeing the nearly empty carafe on the table.

Once the initial frenzy of eating faded, they slowed down as they became sated, picking at morsels in between sips of the crisp white wine. The conversation picked back up.

'So, Sofia, how was your first week with Sublime Retreats?' asked her Father

Her face lit up that her father had remembered the name of the company, and she told them about her week. 'I still have so much to learn,' she finished as she poured some more wine before proffering the jug to her mother. 'Peter, my boss, he's leaving on a big trip next Saturday so I really have to put my head down this week, learn everything I can. I need to manage things for him while he's away.' Her face became pensive at this. She looked down at her empty plate, lost in thought.

'A toast!' Valentina announced suddenly, standing and raising her glass. 'To Sofia, being more than capable of handling her new and very important job. And to my boys, in their new endeavour. Next Saturday is going to be momentous for us all!'

☼

Adam had spent the weekend turning into his Father. He'd gone over on Saturday afternoon to watch the game with him but when he had mentioned Sofia and the visit from her menacing-looking brother, both men had abandoned the TV and become absorbed in the office, going over Jack's files on the bank robbery case. Sunday morning found him sitting in his shorts, with his laptop, searching out more information about the events and the family thought to be involved in the heist, deeply regretting the stuffed crust pizza he'd shared on a whim with his Dad the night before.

Adam was dragged from his research by the ringing of his cell phone. Looking at the screen, it surprised him to see it was Peter; he wasn't a boss who usually interfered with people on the weekend.

With a sense of impending doom, he picked it up and answered, 'Hey Peter, what's up?'

'Adam, I'm so sorry to disturb you,' the man sounded distressed. Adam could hear a hubbub in the background. 'It's Marc, he's been in a terrible car accident,' Peter's voice broke and he paused, trying to control his fears for his husband.

'Oh my God,' said Adam, sitting up straight 'how is he?'

'I don't know the full story. I've only just got to the hospital. They won't let me in to see him yet. Listen, I need you to do me a favour. I left my briefcase in the office, we... we were supposed to be having a work-free weekend together before I leave next week.' There was another pause, which Adam chose not to fill with banalities.

'I understand. You want me to go get it for you?'

'That would be fantastic,' Peter replied, relieved that Adam was so practical and reliable. He gave him the details of what he needed and where they were, saying 'thanks again Adam, I really appreciate this.'

Putting his phone down slowly down on the table, Adam stared at it for a moment, feeling guilty that his primary concern was for the trip to Florence, rather than his poor boss's husband. Pulling himself together, he quickly got dressed and drove uptown to collect Peter's things. It didn't take long being a Sunday; the streets were empty, the office eerily quiet. He felt like an intruder as he padded through to the Director's office, so he stuffed the papers from the in-tray hurriedly into the briefcase and left as quickly as he could.

He found Peter in the waiting room, sitting on one of the hard plastic chairs that seem to be a feature of hospitals worldwide, head in hands, elbows on knees. He looked like a broken man. His face was tear-stained as he looked up in response to Adam saying his name, but he smiled in gratitude at the sight of him.

'Here,' said Adam, passing him the coffee he'd bought on his way up to the floor where Marc was being treated, placing the briefcase on the floor next to Peter's chair.

'You are a lifesaver,' Peter said after drinking down half the coffee in one long gulp.

'Any news yet?' Adam asked

'He's a real mess. They are talking about operating, there's internal bleeding but they want to stabilise him first.'

'I'm so sorry,' Adam replied, putting his hand on Peter's shoulder, giving it a squeeze. 'Marc's a tough cookie, he'll pull through this.' Adam meant it; Marc was a strapping, fit man, despite his soft nature, and if anyone could bounce back after an accident, he was confident it was him.

'You're right, of course,' said Peter, smiling up at him, 'but listen. Whatever happens, you realise this means I won't be going to Italy with you on Saturday?'

Heart sinking, Adam tried to keep his composure; he had so been looking forward to impressing his boss on this trip, really establishing himself as a vital member of the team.

'That's understandable,' he offered, not trusting himself to say anything else.

'But I've thought about it, and the best thing is for you to take Sofia with you instead.'

Adam sputtered out the tea he was sipping on, mind racing in panic.

'I know she's new, but you know what, she's taken to it like a duck to water. She has a superb understanding of how we work and her customer service skills are amazing. On top of that, she speaks Italian. She is Italian. Who better to take with you?'

Scrambling, trying to think of any alternative, the best he could find to say was 'wouldn't it be better for you if she were here?'

Peter shook his head. 'I would be far more comfortable if you had someone else with you. I trust your judgement completely, but it's always good to have a second pair of eyes when viewing properties, you both see different aspects of the place.'

Unable to come up with a single, valid reason for not taking her, Adam resigned himself to the inevitable. 'OK, I'll change the flight tickets when I get back. You want me to let her know?'

'If you could, I'm not sure how long I'm going to be here for. The sooner she knows the better.'

Sofia was helping her Mother clean up after lunch when her phone rang. Seeing an unfamiliar number, she frowned as she answered 'Hello, Sofia speaking.'

'Hi Sofia, it's Adam,' came the reply, causing unexpected butterflies to dance in her stomach.

'Adam, what a surprise,' she managed to say.

'Listen, Peter wanted me to let you know he needs you to go to Florence with me on Saturday.'

Her stomach now lurched for entirely different reasons, and Sofia felt flames of excitement spark inside her. Florence! Her dream destination. She was already mentally preparing the list of places she wanted to see.

'Hello, are you still there?' Adam's voice came down the line.

'Yes, sorry, I was just taken aback is all. Why am I going?'

'Unfortunately, his husband has been in an accident. Peter doesn't think he will be able to get away and feels like you will be a suitable replacement for him.' Adam sounded decidedly unhappy about the new arrangements, but Sofia didn't care about him. She was going to Florence!

'Oh poor Peter, I hope his husband will be OK,' she murmured. The poor man must be beside himself.

'Look, we can have a meeting about this tomorrow, but I will change the names on the tickets today, I'll send through your boarding pass later.'

Putting her phone down she looked at her Mother who was gazing at her expectantly 'what's happening?' Valentina asked, 'are you going somewhere?'

'Yes, Mama, I'm going to Italy, to Florence!' said Sofia, unable to keep the excitement from her face.

'That's wonderful, Bambino. When do you go?'

Sofia was about to answer, then stopped for a moment. 'Oh God, it's on Saturday, I will probably miss the opening party' she looked at her Ma, stricken.

'Now, now, don't fret; let's see what time your flight is. You may be there for some of it. If not,' the woman shrugged, 'so be it. Things always happen for a reason, Sofia.'

Taking comfort from her words, Sofia gave her a quick hug and then ran up to her room to call Suzie and tell her the exciting news.

Adam's next call was to his father to let him know the latest turn of events.

'Well, well, that's very interesting,' said Jack thoughtfully, once he had explained the situation.

'Interesting? I'd say dammed annoying,' retorted Adam peevishly. 'It's totally scuppered my plans; I wanted Peter with me on this trip!'

'I know that, Son, but don't you find it strange that not only does this girl get the job as his assistant but now suddenly she has to go with you to Italy?'

Taken aback, Adam asked curtly, 'what are you talking about, Pa?'

'I have a funny feeling in my waters, Son. Are we sure this accident was just an accident?'

Adam snorted, 'Once a police officer, always a police officer, huh, Pa? Listen, no matter what your spidey senses are telling you, I think this was nothing more than an unfortunate turn of events. We've found no evidence of her family being involved in anything more evil than making a damn fine pizza, have we?'

'I'm just saying be careful, keep your eyes open is all. It may be something and nothing, but I want you to be cautious around this girl, OK?'

☼

The next day in the office, Sofia was all a jitter. They had received an email from Peter confirming that Marc had made it through the surgery and was responding well, which made her feel a little better about her excitement about the upcoming trip. She had received the boarding passes from Adam and printed them off, tucking them in the zippered pocket of her bag for safekeeping.

The twelve-hour fight had a stopover in Amsterdam, another city she would love to see, but they were only there for just over two hours. It had thrilled her to see that the flight was late afternoon, so she would be there for the start of the grand opening of 'ora di pranzo' to support her brothers so they couldn't complain too much.

Walking through to the kitchen to top up with what must be her fourth coffee of the morning, she found Adam there, leaning against the counter with his back to the door, chatting with Anette who she remembered was head of accounts and seemed like a motherly sort of woman.

'Good morning,' she called as she walked in, causing Adam to spin around, knocking over his glass of water with his elbow, splashing it down the front of Anette's shirt.

'Oh God, I'm sorry,' he yelped, grabbing some kitchen paper off the huge roll hanging on the wall, going to dab at it until he realised what he was about to do. He stopped, a terrified look on his face as his hand hovered inches from Anette's chest and he had a flashback to last month's prevention of sexual harassment in the workplace seminar that they had all had to go to. He was pretty sure he was moments away from crossing every boundary they had mentioned.

Seeing his distress, Anette plucked the wad of paper from his trembling hand and smiled her thanks, taking a step back before blotting the front of her shirt. Relieved, Adam's hand flopped down to his side and he could finally respond to Sofia, who had watched the performance with amusement in her eyes. Being a first-class klutz, she relished slapstick when it was happening to someone else, especially as Adam came across as so priggish and distant.

'Sofia,' he squeezed out, 'how are you today?'

'I'm fantastic,' she beamed at him, unaware of the effect it had on him. 'I am so looking forward to our trip. Of course, I'm devastated for Peter, but the thought of travelling to Italy is so exciting. Will I have time to do any sightseeing?'

She placed a cup under the spout, flicking the coffee machine on whilst she was talking, turning to look up at him with this last question. As the smell of the espresso reached him, he suddenly felt the desire to drink some. Coffee was something he had given up years ago, along with most of his favourite foods, in his efforts towards healthy living. A flash of anger ripped through him. This girl seemed to press all the wrong buttons.

'It's a business trip, Sofia, not a vacation. We have a very busy schedule, as you would know if you had bothered to read the itinerary I sent through this morning.'

Sofia flinched and paled; she had glanced at it but was waiting to look at it in detail, discuss it with him when they had the meeting he had mentioned. She felt foolish and ill-equipped, like the first time she had stood on stage to play the violin before an audience. Taking strength from the memory of how well that had turned out despite her fears, the resounding applause confirming what she had already had known, that she had played her piece well, she took a breath before replying to the huffy looking man before her.

'Of course, I have looked at it but I have some questions about it, is all. I wanted to discuss things with you at the meeting you have yet to set up for today.' Looking pointedly at her watch, she continued, 'any idea when you plan for this meeting to happen?'

Anette, who was watching the exchange with feline avidity, smirked and held in a snort, turning to the trash with the now sodden paper to cover her mirth.

Realising he had completely forgotten about the comment he'd made yesterday and that he really should sit down to discuss seriously with her his plans for this trip if he expected her to be of any help to him at all, Adam bit back a retort. Pulling out his phone from his trouser pocket, he checked his schedule for today. There were several Zoom meetings set up with agents; he'd booked out the conference room for the entire afternoon for that purpose. Reluctantly, he realised he would have to ask her to stay after work a little later if they were going to get this done today.

Trying to sound less waspish, he asked, 'do you mind if we meet just before five? It will run over a bit I'm afraid but we have a lot to go through.'

She looked at him long and hard; he looked contrite. But she didn't trust his fickle nature, blowing hot then cold – well, mainly cold if she thought about it. It was the only thing she was dreading about this trip was having to spend time with Adam. He wilted a little under her laser stare, and she softened slightly.

'I tell you what, I'll order us in some food if we are going to be here a while,' she said 'where shall we meet?'

'I'll be in the conference room, most likely,' he said and left without looking at her again.

'God, he creams my corn!' Sofia muttered to herself as she retrieved her coffee, which was cold now.

'You seem to have got under his skin too,' said the all but forgotten Anette, leering at Sofia. 'I've never known him to get so het up about anything.'

'You surprise me,' Sofia replied, taking a sip then discarding the coffee in the sink. 'He's got a stick up his butt that one and no mistake,' as she walked out of the kitchen.

Anette, who was a good deal older and a good deal wiser than either of these two, smiled knowingly to herself. Love was indeed blind, it would seem.

A CAVAL DONATO NON SI GUARDA IN BOCCA

(Don't look a gift horse in the mouth)

An hour before the meeting, Sofia was dithering. She had claimed the pile of takeaway menus from the permanent stack in the kitchen, and they spoiled her for choice. Salivating over each one, her stomach started growling angrily in anticipation. Eventually she just closed her eyes, picking one at random, otherwise she would have been there until the cleaning staff arrived in the dawn. Looking down, she saw she was having Chinese, and casting a prayer up to St Lorenzo that it had been none of the Pizza leaflets in the pile, she discarded the rest, concentrating on what they offered.

Twenty minutes after ordering, the leather-clad delivery man bounded from the elevator with a waft of sweet and sour accompanied by fried pork. Paying him, rewarding him with a tip and one of her brilliant smiles, she took the hefty bag from him and made her way to the conference room, which was at the other end of the office. Pushing open the door, she could hear Adam still on a call so quietly made her way in, placing the food on the table at the back of the airy room, set up to cater for meetings.

Adam had been engrossed in his conversation and not noticed

the girl's entrance but became aware of the scent of eastern promise just before he heard a clink of a plate. Looking around quickly, he threw her a brief smile before wrapping up the call with the agents in San Sebastian, assuring them that he would be in touch in the next few days with more details of Sublime Retreat's requirements. Pushing his glasses back into position on his nose, he stood up to collect his papers together in an orderly fashion and turned his head to talk to Sofia, whilst he put them in his briefcase.

'So, Sofia, are you looking forward to our trip?'

'Are you kidding? It couldn't be a more perfect place for me to go if you tried!'

Adam paused, his father's words echoing back to him. He shook away the crazy thoughts and smiled at her 'I'm glad you are excited. But remember, it's a business trip, not a jolly.'

'I'm not stupid, Adam,' she snapped, glaring at him, banging the carton of rice she was holding down on the table, scattering its contents like confetti.

Realising he was being a jerk again, Adam walked over and stood in front of her, looking down into her face. 'I'm sorry, Sofia,' he said sincerely 'it's just that this trip is a big deal for me. I've been working on this for months, it's the single most important thing I have done since I started here and it absolutely has to be perfect.'

He reached out his hand to touch her arm, and there it was again, that spark of electricity arcing between them. He dropped his hand as Sofia flinched, her beautiful eyes widening in shock. They stood staring at each other mutely for a moment before she rallied her senses.

'Ok, I get that,' she said softly, turning to continue dishing up the food, 'but there's no need to treat me like an idiot.'

He nodded as she glanced back at him 'Fair enough. I promise to try to keep my OCD about this trip under control.'

She laughed at this, causing his heart to skip, and said 'shall we eat?' She had a feeling this man was OCD about everything in his life, from food to work, but at least he was trying. She carried on serving the food, and they both took their plates to the long conference table and settled down to eat.

They spent the next hour discussing the itinerary, Sofia talking between huge mouthfuls of food, Adam merely picking at his. She had ordered everything off the menu that he would have avoided like the plague, but he thought it would be churlish to say so under the circumstances.

'The perfect property has to have all the points on this list,' he said, handing her a sheet of paper 'and then some.'

Sofia scanned the list 'isn't it going to be difficult finding a place in the centre with four beds *and* four bathrooms?' she asked, knowing the old town apartments could be palatial but the luxury of extra bathrooms was rare.

'Yes, it has been an effort,' he replied, pushing his plate to one side, 'but our members dislike sharing facilities, so it's a must-have I'm afraid.'

'You seem to have found a few though,' she said, having flipped the page to see the list of potential properties, and they continued to talk through his planned schedule.

'So, the first few days are going to be pretty full-on,' he finished up, 'but we do need to investigate some of the tours available, so maybe I can leave that to you to look into?'

'Really?' she squealed, bouncing in her chair like a toddler on its way to Disneyland.

'Yes, really' he said, smiling benevolently at her. 'You seem to have a good handle on what's available there, and to be honest, it's the one thing I haven't had time for, I was just going to get some suggestions from the agents whilst we were there.'

'I'd be thrilled to look into that for you,' she said enthusiastically, finally feeling like Adam was treating her like a colleague rather than a hindrance. They stared at each other for a long moment. She saw his irises expand, widening until they almost obliterated the blue, and felt a heat start low down in her body, spreading up and out, blooming like a rose. She stood up abruptly, breaking the connection, busying herself with clearing the plates.

'I'll get onto that first thing tomorrow,' she said, glancing at her watch, 'but now I really have to go. I'm meeting my friend tonight.'

Jumping up to help her collect the debris from their meal, Adam was firmly tamping down the feelings that had been building all the while he had been talking to her. She was gorgeous, funny and so unlike any other woman he had ever met, seeming completely unaware of how attractive he found her. "Pull yourself together, man," he told himself firmly "not only is she ten years younger than you, she's a colleague, a definite no-no." His father's voice popped into his head at that point 'Don't forget she's Mafia Son!' He laughed out loud.

'What's so funny?'

'Oh, I just remembered something my father said earlier, it's not important. Listen, I'll sort this out,' he smiled, taking the plates from her 'you get yourself off to meet your friend and I'll see you tomorrow.'

Not needing to be told twice, Sofia took her leave, making her way quickly to the garage. Sliding into the seat, she expelled a long breath. What was going on with them? She could not deny that she found him attractive, even if he was so prickly. Two weeks in Florence with him was going to be interesting if nothing else!

☼

She met Suzie at their favourite bar along the Seawall Boulevard in Galveston called the Tiki Bar. Its vibrant colours and buzzing atmosphere, along with its frozen margaritas, guaranteed a good time any night of the week. Spotting Suzie perched on a bar stool chatting up her favourite bartender, Carlos, she weaved through the tables, surprising her friend from behind, throwing her arms around her in an enormous hug.

'My God, girl, you nearly made me spill my drink!' Suzie exclaimed when she turned around to see who was grabbing her, before turning her kilowatt smile back to Carlos and drawling, 'another margarita please, honey.' Familiar with Suzie's ways, he laughed good-naturedly and set about dumping ice and the other ingredients into a large blender with practised ease, pouring the delicious result into the prepared frosted glasses with a flourish.

'There you go, ladies, enjoy!' he announced, before moving further down the bar to charm the next group of women patiently waiting for their turn.

Sofia relished her first sip, the ice-cold liquid a welcome relief after the heat of the day and the arduous drive home. 'Oh, that's better,' she exhaled, 'it's been hot as hell today.'

'Come on,' said Suzie, grabbing her bag from the hook under the bar, 'let's go snag a table on the terrace before it gets too busy.'

Following her friend out to the deck and sinking into the chair next to the rustic wooden table, Sofia felt pent up stress leave her body as she looked out to sea. The ocean always made her feel better, and as she sipped again at her drink, she considered her plan to move closer to work. Realising that she would be so much further from the sea put a different slant on her plans.

'So, Florence?' said Suzie, grinning at Sofia over her glass, droplets of melted ice dripping onto the table.

'Yup, I cannot wait.' Sofia replied, automatically reaching for Suzie's glass, now on the table, a damp stain spreading from its base, and sliding a beer mat under it. 'As I said yesterday, I feel dreadful for poor Peter, but it sounds like his husband is doing well. And it has landed this amazing opportunity in my lap. Adam has even asked me to check out some tours, I think he's finally accepting me as someone he can work with,' she grinned happily.

'Adam, the hunky office heartthrob?' Suzie teased, her eyes glinting with amusement.

'Yes, yes,' Sofia answered, knowing full well that denying it was pointless. 'But he blows hot then cold, well, downright icy. He may have started to come round though, I hope so, otherwise this trip will be a nightmare!'

'I'm sure if anyone can charm him it's you, sweetie, you never know, two weeks in one of the most romantic cities in the world...' she left the rest unsaid but arched a perfectly plucked eyebrow at Sofia.

Blushing to the roots of her hair and feeling a frisson of excitement, Sofia tried to refute the suggestion. 'That dog don't hunt, Suzie, he's much older than me and I get the impression he doesn't like me very much. Besides, I work with the guy. It would be crazy. Anyway, he's so busy you'd think he was twins. I don't think he does anything other than work and work out.'

'Well, honey, all I know is that whenever you talk about him, you turn a charming shade of cerise and become more Texan than me. You only start doing that when you're nervous, normally you sound more like Cher in Moonstruck!'

Sofia had to laugh. She knew this was true, she could hear herself doing it and it sounded alien even to her ears. 'Y'all know I just fell off the tater truck, honey,' she replied in her best Texan drawl, causing them both to fall about laughing. Standing up, she said, 'I'll get another round in,' leaving Suzie chuckling to herself.

At the end of the bar, she spotted the recognisable forms of her brothers, so she skipped over to where they were standing. '*Ciao*

Fratelli, what are you plotting?' she asked, causing them to turn and engulf her in a synchronised hug. Once she had extracted herself, she saw Aldo was peering around, obviously looking for her partner in crime.

'Two more please, Carlos,' she called over the bar before saying to the group as a whole, 'Suzie and I are sat outside, you should stop by and say hi.' Causing the younger Marino brothers to snigger like schoolboys - they all knew Aldo had the hots for Suzie as much as she did for him, it was a running joke within the family, bets being placed as to when the two of them would finally figure this out.

'Maybe in a while,' Aldo replied with a grin. 'We're just finalising things for Saturday'

'Everything going to plan?' she asked as Carlos slid over two more frozen Margaritas and she carefully picked them up.

'Sure is Piccolo, I'm glad you'll be there at the start at least, to wish us well.'

'You boys know I will be wishing you well all the way to the airport and all the way to Italy. In fact, the first thing I will do when I land is check your new Instagram account to see all the brilliant pictures of the celebrations.' Antonio, who was unofficially head of marketing for the project, smiled gratefully at her.

'OK, boys,' she said, proffering up the two dripping glasses, 'I'd better get these to the table before they melt completely,' and she left them to their plans, winding her way through the tables and back out to the deck where Suzie was scrolling through her phone. Looking up at the clink of glassware being placed on the table, she said, 'Didja get lost? You were gone ages.'

'Sorry, Suz, ran into my brothers in there, you know what they're like, they beat their own gums to death,' she laughed as she sat back in her seat. They watched the sunset as they sipped their cocktails, chatting about this, that, and nothing much the way that good friends do. The boys stopped by on their way home,

Aldo leading the way, eyes zeroed in on Suzie, who was looking everywhere but at him.

'I hope you're planning to come through and help us celebrate on Saturday, Suzie Q?' he said as he got to the table.

'I'll be there with bells on!' she exclaimed heartily 'wouldn't miss it for the world.' She gave him a special smile that left him speechless. His brothers dragged him away before he could make more of a fool of himself and left the girls to finish their drinks. When darkness finally fell, they collected up the glasses, taking them back to the bar for Carlos, calling thanks and goodbye to him on their way out. Sofia walked Suzie to the end of her road with promises to message her tomorrow and see her on Saturday.

When Sofia climbed into bed that night, she couldn't sleep, even though she was exhausted. Her mind spinning with images of Adam, then Florence, each equally thrilling. When she finally drifted off, it was to a night of disturbed sleep, filled with vivid dreams that she couldn't quite remember in the morning.

☼

The next four days were a flurry of emails, web searches and planning as she worked studiously to find trips for them to trial. Having been given the responsibility, she was determined to show Adam that his trust wasn't misplaced and that he could rely on her to help him make City Breaks a success. She didn't see him, other than at a distance across the office, until Friday afternoon, just as she was getting ready to leave, when he came and found her in Peter's office.

'All set for tomorrow?' he asked with a smile that caused his eyes to crinkle at the edges and her stomach to lurch a little.

'I reckon so.' She replied, slipping her bag over her shoulder as she stood to leave. 'I maybe have packed too much, but other than that I'm ready' she laughed as they walked together towards the elevators.

Nodding in understanding he said, 'it can be tough on these trips, but I guess too much is better than too little!' he stood back to allow her to enter the elevator first. Following her in and pressing the button for the Fitness Suite, and asked which floor she was parked on and then lit that button, too.

'I have arranged for a car to pick you up first, 2 pm from Galveston tomorrow, then they'll swing by to collect me from Pasadena on the way to the airport. Saves us trying to track each other down in the departures hall.'

As he smiled down at her, she became aware of how tall he was, nearly as big as Aldo, and how small the elevator suddenly felt. 'That sounds great,' she murmured. Then, finding her voice, 'in fact, it's perfect. We're having a bit of a party at the restaurant, if a car comes for me they will have to let me leave!'

As she gave him her breathtaking smile, he was saved from trying to find words by the chime announcing they'd arrived at his floor. Hefting his gym bag onto his shoulder, he scuttled out with a quick, 'see you tomorrow then,' over his shoulder, catching her surprised expression as the doors closed once more. Feeling like an idiot, he put himself through a good workout, taking out his frustrations on the bench press until he could barely feel his arms.

☼

On the drive home, Sofia concluded Adam was slightly unhinged, possibly bipolar. Every time she thought she had a handle on him, he said something weird or behaved strangely. How she was going to put up with him for two entire weeks in a foreign country she didn't know, but she was certainly going to be earning her pay check.

Getting ready for bed that night, Sofia felt unsettled. The job with Sublime Retreats was everything she had wanted for so long, and she couldn't quite believe her luck. The trip to Florence was yet another dream come true and she couldn't help fear that something was going to go wrong. '*Tocca Ferro,*' she muttered to herself, touching the iron bedstead to ward off bad luck.

As she tried to get to sleep, Adam's face appeared in her mind, and she remembered again that buzz that ran through her body when they touched. He was very good-looking, no doubt about that. But did she want to get involved with an older man? One that had serious control issues and one that she worked with? She huffed and rolled over in her bed, trying to dislodge these thoughts and get some sleep. Tomorrow was going to be a long enough day without tormenting herself all night.

☼

Adam had arranged to spend Friday night with his dad, as he was going to be away for the next two weeks. He felt a strange mixture of guilt and relief at this thought and conceded easily when Jack insisted on fried chicken for dinner. They sat at the family table in the kitchen when it was delivered, Adam trying to load as much salad as he could onto his plate.

'So, Adam, I've been doing some more digging into Sofia's side of the Marino family,' said his dad, waving a chicken leg, grease glistening on his chin. Gesturing with his napkin at his dad's face, Adam asked, 'found anything interesting?'

'Well, her dad, Giovanni, is the nephew of the Marino thought to be involved in the robbery. But I've checked his photo, there's no way he could be the thin one from that day. Even then, he obviously enjoyed his food,' Jack said with relish as he ripped off another mouthful of chicken.

Chuckling to himself at the irony, Adam said, 'well that puts paid to that then. I know you were hoping to find your missing link there, but it seems to have come to a dead-end.'

'I wouldn't bet on that,' said Jack doggedly, standing to get them both another beer. 'I have a feeling about this. You may dismiss my hunches, but I've never known them to be wrong,' he continued indistinctly as his head disappeared into the fridge.

Deciding to humour the old man, Adam accepted the beer with a smile of thanks and ignored the comment and said instead, 'I'll have to hit the hay after this one. I want an early night so I'm on the ball tomorrow.'

'Aw, I wanted us to watch a movie together as we're going to miss our game-time while you're away,' said Jack with a pout.

Adam considered him for a moment before giving in. 'Ok, Pop, whatcha got in mind?'

With a big grin, Jack leapt up. 'Excellent, we're going to watch The Godfather!' and he trotted through to the lounge to turn on the TV. Chuckling, Adam followed. He had to hand it to him. Not only was he like a dog with a bone once he had an idea in his head, but he'd also picked the longest film he could think of, and Adam knew deep down that it was because he wanted to extend their time together. Adam settled down on his usual chair with a contented sigh, smiling at his dad as the credits came up before they both became lost in the story.

UN PO' DI GELOSIA

(A little bit of jealousy)

From: Peterwilliams@sublimeretreats.com

To: Adamflynn@sublimeretreats.com

CC: Sofiamarino@sublimeretreats.com

Subject: Italy Product Trip

Dear Adam and Sofia,

I just wanted to reach out and wish you luck for the trip to Italy. I hope all goes smoothly, and it is successful all-around!

I also wanted to express my gratitude for your adept handling of the whole situation after the unfortunate events last week. Marc is doing well; I hope they will let him come home this weekend so I can look after him properly. Knowing the City Breaks program is in such capable hands makes this a lot easier for me –thank you both.

As ever, I am available if you need anything, please just let me know.

Best regards,

Peter

Peter Williams

General Manager–Sublime Retreats

The kitchen was already a hive of industry the next morning when Sofia eventually surfaced. She had luxuriated in what would probably be her last lie-in for some time, before padding downstairs for her coffee.

'Finally, you are awake, *Piccolo*!' called Aldo as he scurried past her, laden with bunting and packets of balloons in the colours of the Italian flag. 'Can you help me blow these up?' he called back through the swinging doors.

'Give me a minute to wake up,' she yelled after him as she walked over to the industrial coffee machine to set it in motion. Her Mother bustled in with armfuls of shopping, dumping the bags on the side.

'Oh, please make me a cup, Sofia,' she said, plucking out items and deftly putting them away. 'Your brothers are acting like we've never served a meal in our lives.' she laughed. 'But it's good to see them so excited about this, I hope it works!'

'I'm sure it will be amazing,' Sofia replied, placing the coffee on the counter next to her. 'They have been working hard on the promotion; it's been getting a brilliant response.'

'And you must be excited, too? Today is your big day, off on your fancy business trip to Italy!'

Sofia grinned. It still didn't feel real, even though she was all packed and had her boarding passes.

'Don't forget to call Uncle Joey when you get there, he's thrilled that you are going to be in Florence. He says he will take you for dinner.'

Remembering Adam's snarky comments about it being a work trip, Sofia wasn't entirely sure she could go gadding about with her uncle, but she had missed him desperately since he returned to his home country and she was determined to find a way.

'Yes, Mamma, of course. I'm looking forward to seeing him.'

There was a loud crash from the restaurant followed by language that caused her mother to frown in disapproval. 'Don't worry, Mamma, I'll go,' Sofia said quickly, racing through to see what the hullabaloo was about.

She was greeted by the sight of her five brothers looking mournfully down at the remnants of what had been the cake, shaped like Italy, to launch their flavours of the home country specials. Luka and Flavio looked sheepish, so she guessed they were the cause of the splattered confection.

Aldo, with a half-blown balloon in one hand, let forth a stream of abusive comments which had them all standing back under its force. Sofia giggled. She couldn't help it. Aldo looked ridiculous with his ferocious face, waving around a wilting red balloon.

The boys all turned at the sound of her snorting, trying to keep the laughter in check, but it was infectious. One by one they grinned. Even her big brother eventually caved and smirked.

'Right, boys,' she said, looking at the twins, 'you get this cleared up. Aldo, I'm just gonna get dressed and then I can lend you a hand with those.' She pointed at the vast pile of balloons on the table next to him. It looked like he had enough to completely cover the walls. 'I will also call Suzie and tell her to swing by PattyCakes Bakery on her way here. How many people are you expecting?'

Antonio responded happily, 'at least fifty people have said they're coming so my guess there will be more than that.'

Sofia nodded, 'OK, leave it with me, and try not to balls anything else up while I get dressed.'

Two hours later, they were ready. The restaurant looked fantastic, and her brothers had retreated to the kitchen to finish the prep work on the food. Sofia sank into a booth for a few moments of peace while she waited for Suzie to arrive with the emergency cake. She had been so caught up in helping them get ready, she hadn't had time to overthink the upcoming trip.

Giovanni, who had been noticeable by his absence that morning, came through the front door, clutching a gift bag in one hand, stopping in his tracks when he registered the decorated space that was his restaurant.

'*Ammazza!*' he said, looking about in wonder 'they have been busy, huh?'

Sofia was happy to see he looked impressed rather than disturbed at the transformation, and patted the seat next to her. 'Come, Papà, tell me what you have been up to today whilst we've been busy like hot grease on a skillet?' Smiling at her, he chose to sit on the seat opposite her so he could look at her, sliding the gift bag across the table as he did so.

'This is for you, Sofia, a little something to keep you safe on your journey.'

Surprised, Sofia pulled the pretty bag towards her and upended its contents on the table. A tissue-wrapped package fell out, and she carefully separated the pink paper to reveal a beautiful, silver charm bracelet. She looked up at her Father, not sure how to respond.

'Look at the charm,' he said with a smile and gestured towards the bracelet. She held it cupped in her left hand, turning over the small disc dangling from it with her right, breaking into a smile when she recognised the form of St. Lorenzo etched onto it.

'I thought you could get more charms from your travels around the world to put on it,' he said, gazing at her intently. Looking into his dark, heavyset eyes, she understood this was his way of giving his blessing to her endeavours to strike out into the world and she choked up, eyes filling she struggled for something to say.

'*Papà*, it's gorgeous. Although I'm not sure the patron saint of cooks has any influence on travelling but I love it!'

'Have you forgotten what day it is? It's the 10th of August, his feast day, in Florence they will celebrate him today,' the old man said with a glint in his eye 'I can't think of anyone better to look after my little girl as she travels there.'

Awed at the thought he'd put into the gift, Sofia was saved from completely losing it by the noise of Suzie arriving. Banging the front door open with her butt, bearing a large cake box, tottering on heels she didn't need. She looked absolutely stunning. Giovanni's jaw dropped at the sight of her. She was wearing a simple, blue sheath dress the same shade as her eyes and her dirty blonde hair was skilfully held in a chignon, thick braids running down the sides. Sofia jumped up to take the cake box from her with a smile; she knew exactly who all this glamour was for.

'Suzie, you are a lifesaver,' she said as she put the packet on the table and turned to hug her, having to reach up higher than usual. Standing back to admire her friend's outfit, she took in the never-ending legs and thought that poor Aldo was going to have his socks knocked off today and no mistake. 'Come, take a seat. What can I get you to drink?'

'A white wine spritzer, please, lots of ice,' said Suzie, slumping into the seat that Sofia had vacated. 'Morning, Giovanni,' she added politely. Giovanni was still in shock. He still thought of Sofia and her friend as little girls. It seemed he would never adjust to seeing them as women. Standing to take the cake somewhere for safekeeping, he said, 'Good morning, Suzie, thank you for coming to support the boys today.'

'Wouldn't miss it for the world!' she replied, gratefully taking her drink from Sofia, letting its chilled form cool her hands before taking a sip. No sooner had Giovanni disappeared through the swing doors into the kitchen, they swung back the other way to reveal Aldo, who'd seen the cake box and knew that meant Suzie had arrived.

'Suzie Q,' he called in the teasing childhood way that used to annoy her so much '*Grazie mille* for going to the baker's for us…'

he stopped, staring at her as she rose from her seat to greet him. Sofia giggled to herself behind the bar as the Disney moment played itself out in front of her. There should be bluebirds twittering around their heads, surely?

Suzie, standing self-consciously under his awestruck gaze, shifted from one foot to another 'it was my pleasure' she voiced breathlessly and they both moved in at the same time for the traditional cheek kissing, bumping heads awkwardly in the process. Aldo, spotting her drink on the table, leapt at something to distract from the situation.

'*Piccolo*, why does she not have an Aperol Spritz? You know that is our drink for today!' he blustered, coming around the bar, pushing her unceremoniously out of the way while he prepared the correct drink.

Sofia winked as she popped herself down opposite Suzie, who had sunk gladly back into her seat, still slightly flushed. 'Seems like you had the desired effect,' she whispered across the table.

'What do you mean?' Suzie responded, having the decency to look guilty as charged.

'Really? You're still gonna play that game?' she hissed back at her friend 'you and I both know you have the hots for my big brother!'

'You're a fine one to talk. You and I both know you have the hots for this Adam, but I don't see you doing anything about it!'

'That's different,' said Sofia, looking away from Suzie, twisting her rings. She had been trying not to let her imagination run away with her about a possible romance with that annoying man.

'I don't see how. This is the first time I've seen you interested in anyone for years. When was the last time you had a date? That guy in college, what was his name, Douglas?'

Sofia nodded, returning her gaze to Suzie 'I'm... I'm not as confident around men as you, Suzie' she continued, sotto voiced, hoping her friend wouldn't take this conversation any further. She didn't want anyone to know just how uncomfortable she was with the idea of getting close to a man, any man.

Composure returned, Aldo strode over, placing two tall glasses containing the beautiful amber liquid that was to be his signature drink for the day on the table, ice clinking and orange slices bobbing invitingly. Both girls looked up at him with a smile, picked up the drinks and said *'Saluti'* before taking their first, tentative sips.

'Wow, that's good,' said Suzie 'you will have to drink these with Adam in Florence,' she added cattily, but with a grin to let her know there was no malice involved. Looking at her watch, Sofia said to her brother, 'it's nearly twelve, Aldo, time for kick-off. I'll hold the fort here while you go get changed and check our brothers haven't done anything else stupid.' He laughed and plonked a kiss on the top of her head before taking her advice and heading to the kitchen, Suzie's gaze burning holes in his jeans as he retreated.

Shaking her head in amusement, Sofia cleared away the discarded wine spritzer before going to prop open the front door in welcome, ready for the first party guests. It didn't take long before the place started to fill up, friends and family alike coming to enjoy their hospitality. As Sofia stood watching over the event, her mind already jumping ahead to the plane, she was happy to notice unfamiliar faces. They had attracted new customers, which was exactly what they wanted. She caught Antonio's gaze from the far side of the room where he was chatting to some girls and gave him a thumbs up. He grinned back at her, happy with the results from his marketing efforts.

Seeing that it was approaching 2 pm, Sofia slipped out unnoticed to go up to get her suitcase and pop her final bits and pieces in her carry-on bag. Looking around her room to make sure she had forgotten nothing, she felt a pang of... what? Homesickness already? This was going to be the longest time she would be away from her home and her family, which was ridiculous at her age, but it was a fact. It was quite daunting. She hadn't quite comprehended how much she relied on them for support. She knew whatever happened in her life, she could count on her family to be in her corner, whether she was right or wrong. Being away from that unequivocal reinforcement was going to be strange. Giving herself a shake to dislodge any fears, she pulled her backpack on and grabbed the handle of her bright red suitcase, hauling it down the stairs with an ungainly crablike gait.

Leaving her bags just inside the doors of the kitchen for easy access, she walked back into the party, which was in full swing now. With music playing, people were standing in groups, chatting. The place felt alive for the first time in years.

Finding her parents sitting at the corner table with a group of their cronies, she squeezed in next to her mother to spend her last few minutes with them before her ride arrived. Too soon she saw a large silver car glide up outside and a besuited driver climb out and stand by the vehicle. Gulping, she stood up. Her parents followed, calling to Flavio and Roberto who were nearest to fetch her luggage. There followed the inevitable tearful scene on the pavement outside the restaurant as every member of her family insisted on hugging her goodbye, each giving her a pearl of worldly wisdom to take with her.

'Don't sit under the air-conditioning, you'll catch pneumonia'

'Don't sleep in any bed with your feet facing the door, you'll die'

Don't put a hat on the bed, that's unlucky too.'

'Don't swallow a watermelon seed, they grow inside you!'

'Don't drink cold water unless you want a terrible sore throat.'

'Don't sit in rows thirteen or seventeen on the planes.'

The list was endless; she let it wash over her in a wave of love and good intentions as it was intended. Finally, Suzie, who had been listening with amusement, was standing in front of her and was allowed to say her piece.

'Do have a wonderful time, do go see everything you want to see and do follow your heart.' She hugged her swiftly, then pushed her towards the impatient looking driver, 'gonna miss ya girl, keep me posted!' she called before ushering the group back into the party.

Sinking into the cool climate of the car, Sofia grinned. She was already sitting in the air conditioning; there was no hope for her! In the hour-long drive to Pasadena, she felt excitement building with every mile that passed, her stomach lurching every time she thought of the journey ahead. Reaching down to take a small bottle of water thoughtfully provided by the transfer company, she giggled out loud as she felt its icy temperature "strike two!" she thought to herself but took the chance and drank it anyway, trying to numb the effects of the two Aperol Spritzers that had been foisted upon her despite her best intentions. She looked out the window with interest as the car pulled to a stop outside a well-tended suburban house. The driver repeated his movements of earlier, slipping out and standing to attention by the passenger door.

She saw the front door open and Adam stuck his head out, waving to show he was on his way and within a few minutes he reappeared, trundling what looked like a tiny case behind him. She heard the muted murmur of his greeting to the driver through the glass, felt the car shift slightly as they opened the trunk to receive his luggage, and then firmly shut it.

It surprised her when the passenger door opened, revealing Adam, who slid in next to her. For some reason, she had assumed he would sit upfront. 'Hey Adam,' she said, looking at his still-damp hair and slightly dishevelled look, 'everything OK? Is this where you live?'

He looked a little taken aback, but ran his hand through his hair and replied, 'Yes, all good. Overslept a little is all. And no, I don't live here; it's my parents' house. I wanted to spend some time with my father before we left.'

'That's sweet,' she said, noticing him colour slightly at her words.

'How was the party?'

'Fab, thank you. I left them still at it. There was a great crowd; it will be good for the business.'

'Are you involved much? In the "family business"?' he asked with a strange emphasis which caused her to frown slightly.

'I help out where I can' she replied, looking at him quizzically, her eyebrows raised, her pert little mouth puckered up in a way he found enchanting. Looking away quickly, he strove for a change of topic.

'We'll be there in good time. We can get our bags checked in then grab a coffee or something if you'd like?'

'Sounds good. I've had a busy day already so I need a little pick-me-up. I don't want to miss a moment of this trip.'

'Take my advice, sleep whenever you can. Your system will not know whether it's coming or going in these next days, it's seven hours ahead in Italy.'

'Oh, I've had more than enough advice for one day. You wouldn't believe my family's ideas. That reminds me, do you know which row we're sitting in? My paperwork is in the bag in the trunk.'

He cocked his head to one side, thinking. 'Mine too. I don't recall which row though, does it matter?'

'Probably not,' she smiled 'I was just curious.'

The final half-hour of the drive to George Bush Intercontinental passed mostly in silence, both of them wrapped in their thoughts. Adam mentally running through the arrangements, which he now knew by heart, for the next few days, and Sofia's thoughts swinging between wonderful Florence and the people she'd left behind. The airport was heaving; they were obviously flying at a busy time, so it took quite a while to get checked in. By the time they'd made it through security, Sofia felt exhausted and was looking forward to a coffee.

It was only when she'd struggled onto one of the uncomfortable, tall stools that airports worldwide seem to favour, whilst Adam went to get their order, that she remembered to check the boarding passes to see what rows they would be sitting in.

'Well, whaddaya know,' she said to herself, looking at the two bits of paper.

'What's up?' said Adam, placing their drinks on the table and sitting on his stool, his height making him a little more graceful than she had been.

'We're in row thirteen to Amsterdam, then row seventeen to Florence. *Oddio! La sfortuna,*' she added in a whisper, involuntarily crossing herself before kissing her fingers. Stirring his skim chai latte, Adam frowned.

'I can understand why thirteen might not be popular, but what's wrong with row seventeen?' he asked, taking his first tentative sip.

'Oh, in Italy the number seventeen is much worse than thirteen,' she said seriously. 'Something to do with the Roman numerals referring to the end of your life in Latin.'

'You don't really believe that claptrap, do you?' he asked with a smirk on his face that made her want to slap it right off.

'Listen, you' she started, but he held up his hand to shush her, head cocked to one side as he listened to an announcement. His face paled slightly.

'What? What did they say?'

'Our flight is delayed,' he replied slowly, looking at her with concern. 'Oh God, we might miss our connection. This could screw everything up!' His voice was rising hysterically by this point, causing the people at the next table to look round.

'Calm down, Adam,' she said evenly. 'I'll ignore the fact that you were just being sarcastic about our seats being unlucky, for now. How long did they say the delay was?'

'Estimated forty minutes... At the moment. I don't like the "estimated", they always say that when they're not sure.'

He looked down into his cup as if he was looking for portents. Sofia smiled; he looked like a little boy who'd lost his favourite toy.

'Well, let's not panic just yet. If they're not sure, it may even get here before that. Let's go to the gate, we can get more up-to-date information from there.' She finished her espresso and slid off her stool. 'Come on!' she said as she pulled her backpack into place, as he hadn't moved a muscle.

Realising she was right, he pushed his unfinished drink to one side and followed her to their gate.

The seating area was a mass of bodies. The air was buzzing with hundreds of concerned voices; all wanting to know what was going on. Adam looked around, unable to make sense of the mess before him. He followed Sofia who had surged ahead, ignoring the queue, and who was now talking to the beleaguered desk agent. The young man was startlingly good looking, his uniform fitting a body that worked out regularly like a glove. He took one look at Sofia and seemed to snap to attention.

Adam, who'd been in this situation many times, was surprised; the gate guardians usually had their armour of cool disinterest in place to deal with these situations. He watched as Sofia leaned in, telling the young man something. He saw the eyes flash in recognition and a winning smile appear on his previously passive face. Whatever she had said seemed to animate the man. Shortly after, she approached Adam and told him 'looks like it will be about an hour delayed, but we should still make our connection' she smiled at him, assuming that her words would reassure him.

'Why is that "boy" giving you information?' he snapped, unaware of where his anger was coming from but unable to ignore the hot burning sensation in his gut.

Despite flinching at his words, Sofia felt compelled to explain, 'He's one of my brother's classmates, and he recognised me and wanted to help.'

'Oh, I bet your "family" knows everybody to some extent?' he taunted.

'What does that mean exactly?' she demanded, tired now of his riddles and his snippy attitude.

Realising he was sounding like a spoilt brat, Adam took a moment before answering. Taking off his glasses, he rubbed his eyes with his thumb and forefinger. 'Sorry, it's nothing. Just ignore me. I'm stressed, is all. I shouldn't be taking it out on you,' he offered with a small smile.

'Well, then…' she looked around, and spotting some empty seats, nodded in their direction. 'Go grab us those seats. I'm just going to nip to the bathroom.' He watched her retreating form for a moment; he had to pull himself together. He was supposed to be in charge on this trip, but he'd lost his cool at the first hurdle, a minor one at that. She was breezing through it with aplomb. Seeing another group entering the waiting area, he hurried to grab the seats that Sofia had spotted, claiming the empty one next to him for her with his carry-on bag.

She returned with two bottles of water, giving him one without a word before sitting down when he pulled his bag onto the floor by his feet. There was a strained silence, both of them feigning interest in people-watching, trying to think of something to say.

'So,' they both said, making them laugh awkwardly and breaking the ice a little. 'You go,' he said gallantly, leaning in, nudging her with his shoulder playfully. Very aware of the heat of his body so close to hers, Sofia's brain scrambled. She hadn't really had a conversational gambit in mind when her mouth had opened of its own accord.

'Ok. Tell me something about yourself. Who is Adam Flynn, what makes him tick?'

'There's not much to tell, really, you saw my family's house,' he smiled at her. 'That's where I grew up. My pop was a police officer, but he's retired now. My ma did work before she had me but then became a full-time mum. She was great at it too,' he said sadly. Picking up on his tone, she looked at his profile as he gazed across the room. 'Was?' she asked quietly. She saw him rapidly blinking before saying 'yeah, she died a while ago now.'

'I'm sorry, Adam, that's tough. I can't imagine how that must feel. Were you close?'

He turned his head and gave her a sorry smile 'yeah we were. I was always much closer to her than Pop; he was never around much, what with shift work and all. So Ma and me were the dynamic duo. She was always there for me, you know?'

'Sounds like my mom. My entire family, actually' she wondered how the party was going and if Aldo had picked up the courage to ask Suzie out yet.

'That sounds kinda cool. I always wondered what it would be like to have brothers or sisters, must be great to have that group support.'

'Not always,' she said with a grin, 'some days I want to slap the lot of them and they drive me crazy.'

As Sofia continued to regale him with stories of the tricks her brothers had played on her growing up, they settled into an easy conversation, leaning into each other, unaware of the shift in the dynamic. Before they knew it, the chimes that preceded announcements sounded and they were informed that their flight had landed and they should prepare for boarding shortly.

Watching the mad dash of passengers, determined to be at the front of the queue and board the plane first, Adam pointed at the growing line, saying, 'I have never understood why people feel the need to do that. We're all going to take off at the same time' he laughed, shaking his head.

'FOMO,' she replied, obviously as amused as he was.

'What the giddy heck is that?' he asked. It amazed Sofia that he hadn't heard of the phrase, so she explained and discovered that, apart from LinkedIn, he didn't have any social media accounts. 'That is just plain weird.' she said, as they stood to join the queue which was now moving 'we've gotta get you set up on Instagram. You could do a lot of promotion for the company on there, especially on this trip. You can start building excitement about the City Breaks program right now!'

He loved her enthusiasm for everything; food, work, life. All things seemed to ignite her. She was so passionate about everything. A small part of his brain wondered how passionate she would be in bed. A picture of her naked, lying in his bed with her beautiful dark hair fanned over the pillow, popped into his head. Flushing at his lascivious thoughts, he pushed the image away and tried to refocus on the conversation.

'To be honest, Tim from the media department has been badgering me about that, but I think he's given up now. Listen, I'm not good with this kind of thing. Would you help me? Set up an… Instagram, is it?'

She giggled as they reached the front of the line, handing her passport and boarding pass to the check-in agent to scan. 'God you sound like my Grandpa, how old are you anyway?' and the flash of her smile as she glanced back at him before taking her documents back left him weak at the knees. Not wanting to shout his age across to where she was waiting for him by the tunnel that led to their plane, he waited until his paperwork was scanned so he could join her before answering. 'Only 35, despite sounding like an old codger. I just never got into that stuff; I've always been more focused on what is happening in my life. College, then work, that's what takes up my time.'

To Sofia, it didn't sound like Adam Flynn ever had much fun. His life sounded totally boring, and she'd seen the way he religiously ate only healthy foods, working out on a regular basis. It all seemed regimented somehow, devoid of any pleasure. It couldn't be further from her erratic, spontaneous life, which was filled with laughter, fun, and food, lots and lots of food! Maybe she could show him on this trip that life didn't need to be so orderly, so reliant on a calendar, endless calorie counting.

If you couldn't live *la dolce vita* in Florence, a city full of passion, artwork and amazing restaurants, then there was no hope for you. Decided on her plan, she realised she could use the Instagram account as a means to lead him astray. She knew he would do anything for work and if she convinced that him having a vibrant, fun-filled feed would boost his ratings in the company, he wouldn't be able to refuse.

CHI DORME NON PIGLIA PESCI

(You snooze, you lose)

Her idea kept her entertained while they waited patiently to board and make their way to row thirteen. The people who'd been in such a desperate hurry to board now seemed intent on taking their own sweet time getting settled, blocking the aisle for anyone else. When the large businessman in front of her finally retrieved everything he needed from his briefcase and stowed it away in the baggage compartment, knocking her with it, she cursed under her breath but gave him a dazzling smile, determined not to be as rude as him.

The man found himself smiling in return and making his apologies for holding things up. Observing this interaction, Adam couldn't help but admire her. The effect she had on people, men in particular, was quite remarkable. It was as if she were charmed. They found their seats, and Sofia sidestepped in, taking her place happily by the window. Adam claimed his space next to her and strapped himself in. He immediately pulled the safety card out of the pocket of the seat in front and began noting where the emergency exits were. Sofia, who'd pulled out the inflight magazine, was avidly flicking through to see what it offered.

'When do they feed us?' she asked Adam, who was now looking ahead, watching the final passengers struggle on board with oversized bags that he felt sure did not match the airline's specifications.

'Do you ever stop thinking about food?' he asked with a grin.

'I do, but my stomach doesn't! I'm as hungry as a hog and this flight is what, ten hours?'

'Yes, it's about that, but don't worry. As soon as the seat belt light goes off, they will start serving dinner.'

The captain came over the speaker, asking the cabin crew to prepare for take-off, and they efficiently made their way down the aisle, closing overhead cupboard doors, re-jigging the bags inside to fit and checking that all the passengers had their belts on, seats up and tables folded away. Adam was pleased to note the seat next to him remained empty. He could move over once they'd taken off to give them both more space.

As the plane made its way slowly down the tarmac and turned to wait for its turn for take-off, he saw that Sofia had fallen quiet and was twisting her rings, something he'd noticed she did when she was nervous.

'You OK?' he asked 'don't you like flying?'

Her face was pale, and she looked at him with luminous eyes. 'I don't know, I've never been on a plane before.'

He was taken aback; it hadn't occurred to him that she might not have flown somewhere. It was an alien concept to him as his lack of social media was to her. The plane juddered, then began picking up speed as it built up its momentum to take off. Sofia's hand gripped the armrest between them, knuckles white, her face drawn. Pointing to the bracelet he'd noticed earlier, he said, 'that's nice, is it new?'

She nodded, 'Yes, it was a gift from my dad, to wish me luck on my travels.' She looked down at it fondly, then, loosening her grip a little, pulled it around so he could see the charm. 'This is St. Lorenzo,' she told him 'patron saint of cooks. Well, and the poor, and libraries, but my family prefer the cooks part obviously.' He could see that she was relaxing and unaware that the wheels had just left the ground, so he asked, 'why is he considered the saint of cooks?'

'Well, he was killed protecting the books of the church, but they grilled him to death.' She pulled a face of distaste 'although he is claimed to have said, "turn me over, this side is done" which is where the cooking part comes in I guess. That's why he's always depicted holding a grill, as well as a book. Look.'

She held her arm up for him to examine the charm; he carefully took the tiny disk in his fingers and scrutinised it, noticing a scent rising from her wrist. The smell of jasmine reminded him of his mother; it had been her favourite plant. It still grew in abundance in the backyard of their home. His pa had never much been one for gardening and had left it untended, it was taking over the space with gusto. He let the charm drop and smiled at her. 'I recognise the name, isn't there a church called that in Florence?'

'Yes, it's actually the oldest church there. We'll be seeing it on one of the tours I've set up, the market bears his name too, as does the cooking school, unsurprisingly,' she added with her usual grin, he saw that the colour had returned to her cheeks and the spark was back in her eyes.

'You realise we are up in the air, don't you?' He asked, matching her grin with his. 'We took off a few moments ago.' Her mouth formed an O shape, and she looked out the window to confirm that it was true and saw the earth miles away below them. She looked back at him, realising he had been distracting her. She hadn't mentioned the fact that she'd never flown before, because she thought he would find it amusing and tease her about it. Instead, he'd been thoughtful and kind, which was a side of him she hadn't seen before.

Turning back to look into his handsome face, she found herself almost nose to nose with him. He had leaned forward to look around her at the view out of the window. They both paused, inches away from each other, gazing into each other's eyes. His startling blue transfixed with her liquid brown, neither able to look away. There was a ping as the seatbelt light went off and a commotion as people leapt to their feet for that urgent, forgotten item in their bags overhead or to dash to the toilets. They drew apart, busying themselves with unbuckling their belts and tried to avoid eye contact, lest they got stuck again.

Adam was having a long, hard chat with himself. Not only were his feelings for this girl inappropriate, but he had also sworn off women years ago. Losing his mother had cut him like a knife. He couldn't bear to go through that feeling of abandonment and soul-crushing grief again. Adamant he would let no one else be that important to him, that losing them would make him lose control, he kept things orderly and never wanted people to see him overreact or break down for any reason. He knew some people found him cold, a little distant, but it was his armour, a shield of protection from those feelings you couldn't control.

As promised, when the seatbelt light went out the cabin crew started bustling around up front and soon the smells of cooking, or reheating, she guessed, were tantalising Sofia, taking her mind off Adam. Letting her mind run through the incredible logistics of feeding three hundred people simultaneously from a tiny kitchen space allowed her to ignore the fact that, despite her best intentions, she was becoming more and more attracted to this man. Behind his closed-in demeanour and rigid work ethic, she could sense there was more to him, someone else trying to get out, and she had the feeling she would like to help release his other self.

This was something new to her; she'd never felt like she was getting close to any guy, or even felt the desire to. The few dates she'd been on had been fun, but not anything she'd ever wanted to take further. And even if she had, none of her dates would have passed muster with her brothers, so she had never taken them home. If she'd left home, gone to college out of state, things might have turned out differently, but she'd succumbed to the will of the family and accepted a place in the college closest to Galveston. So that had been that.

Avidly watching the carts being pushed up the aisle, she willed them to hurry. She hadn't eaten at the party even though the food had all looked fabulous, so now her stomach was making its complaints felt. A low growl emerged, causing her to look at Adam in embarrassment. He was pretending not to have noticed and looking straight ahead, but she could see a small smile playing around his lips. The eye that she could see had tell-tale laughter creases in the corner. Yes, he really was quite delicious, she thought to herself. Luckily he only thinks of me as a colleague, otherwise we'd both be in trouble!

Her childlike delight in the meal that was served entertained Adam more than it should. 'Everything is sooo tiny!' she crowed, unwrapping the various sections with the excitement of Christmas morning, tasting morsels in no particular order, making him itch to tell her which sections came first and that the cake was supposed to be dessert. But he refrained and tried to join in with her joie de vivre, allowing her to take snaps of him eating, apparently for his Instagram feed.

Why anyone would be interested in a plate of food was beyond him, but as he looked around, he observed quite a lot of people were taking shots of their meals rather than eating them. It was all quite bizarre. Allowing himself a few mouthfuls of the chicken a la crème before making inroads into the salad, he watched out of the corner of his eye as she practically hoovered the whole thing up without pause for breath. It was a remarkable sight. All the women he knew from work or at the gym seemed to live on lettuce leaves and juices or the occasional protein bar. Yet here was this girl happily devouring everything in sight and washing it down with a nice Cabernet without a care in the world.

The only other woman he had known to enjoy food this much had been his mum, she had loved to cook and eat. His happiest memories with her were in the kitchen, watching her create wonderful meals, delicious cakes, her letting him lick out the bowl. Unfortunately, it was her love of food that had led to her illness, diabetes, and ultimately her death. On the day of her funeral he swore to himself he would never eat that way again. Eschewing all cakes and desserts and any high-fat foods had been his way of coping with his grief, punishing himself for not taking better care of her.

As he lay down his cutlery, Sofia looked disapprovingly at the food left on his tray. Debating whether she could manage another bread roll, she decided she couldn't and startled him by picking up his bread and kissing it, before placing it reverently back in its section on the tray. She saw him staring at her strangely and flushed prettily.

'Sorry. It's a thing. Bread is sacred so should be given the love and attention it deserves; throwing it away is something of a crime to my family.'

He laughed, 'fair enough, I can't say anything. The Irish cut a cross on the top of their bread to let the devil out. We all have our foibles,' he said and picked up her tray to give to the flight attendant who was passing through collecting them. Once their tables were pushed up into place, they both settled back in peaceful silence. Sofia found her eyes growing heavy. She fought against the tiredness for as long as she could but eventually succumbed, falling into a deep, dreamless slumber.

Adam stared at her sleeping face, examining every contour, wondering what it was about her that he found so appealing. Yes, she was pretty and had a smile that could light up a room, but there were plenty of women with those attributes. There was something else, indefinable, an essence of spirit that lifted his soul in a way he found hard to ignore.

But ignore it he must, so he dragged his eyes away and, fairly certain she was out for the count, pulled the tattered copy of the book his father had insisted he read, out of his bag. Galveston's Maceo Family Empire was dog-eared proof that his pop had re-read it many times. It was a factual report on a great crime family's hold on Galveston and their forty-year rule there. He soon found himself absorbed in the story of the brothers from Sicily who came from nothing but created an empire for themselves.

An hour into the book, he felt Sofia shift next to him. Her head slid onto his shoulder. Putting the book down on his lap and reaching across with his left hand, he made to shift her gently back the other way. He couldn't do it. She looked so peaceful, and it felt quite nice, so he left her resting there and continued reading. He must have dozed off himself because the next thing he knew a flight attendant was asking the row in front if they wanted wine with their meal. Looking at his phone, he saw they were 9 hours into the flight and would land in an hour or so.

Putting his book, which had fallen to his lap, back in his bag, he turned slightly, gave Sofia a gentle shake and called her name. She came to blearily, taking in her surroundings. When she registered her head on his shoulder, she sat up smartly, 'God, I'm sorry, I didn't mean to pass out on ya like that!'

'It's fine,' he said with a smile 'I didn't mind. Although the snoring was pretty hard to take.'

Sofia looked mortified; it was only when he started laughing she realised he was yanking her chain and tutted at him.

'I didn't think you'd want to miss the next round of food,' he said, indicating the trolley that was pulling up alongside them. She brightened at the sight of it, humiliation forgotten in an instant, sitting up further, like a dog waiting for its bowl. The last hour of the flight passed quickly and soon the seatbelt light was back on and they were descending into Schiphol Airport. From above, the airport looked like a mutant DNA cell with strands striking out from the sides.

As the flight was late, they were told an agent would be waiting when they disembarked, for those with connecting flights, to give them their gate numbers. Adam looked at the time again 'we've got fifty minutes,' he said earnestly to Sofia. 'It's going to be a push but we should make it.' Nodding, she collected her things together, and they both stood as soon as they could, waiting impatiently for the rows ahead to move. Once they made it into the aisle, they pushed forward as politely as they could, but with a growing sense of urgency. It seemed to take forever. The sense of pressing need they'd seen to board the plane seemed to have dissipated, the same people now in holiday mode and taking their time.

They flew down the tunnel that connected the plane with the building, dodging and weaving between the meanderers until they reached the doors to the airport and located the airline agent with the connection information. The tall blonde had a strangely immobile face one usually associated with Botox and seemed unconcerned about their plight. 'You will board at gate G9,' she said disinterestedly, waving vaguely at the map on the wall. Rushing up to the map they found the dot that showed 'you are here.' They looked at each other in horror. The map let them know they were on Pier B. Pier G couldn't be further away, and of course their gate was right at the end. They shouldered their bags without a word and began sprinting toward their gate.

"Running through an airport should be an Olympic sport," Sofia thought to herself as they ran hell for leather, crashing into discarded trolleys and leaping over suitcases, thoughtlessly blocking the aisles. The fact that Adam was much fitter than her soon became apparent as he forged ahead, only slowing when he realised she was lagging. 'Come on, Sofia,' he called urgently, and she tried to up her speed. Maybe that last meal on the plane had been a bad idea. Sweat was pouring down her face, and she was finding it hard to take a breath.

When she arrived at the gate, she bent over, winded, and tried to regain her composure. They'd made it! It was all she could do to stand straight, handing her boarding pass to the woman at the gate with a shaky arm, and stagger slowly along another tunnel. She realised Adam was supporting her and smiled gratefully at him as they boarded. When they reached row seventeen, she didn't give a hoot how unlucky it was, flopping into her seat with relief.

'That was awful,' she said to him as she strapped herself in. 'Is flying always this stressful?'

'Not always, but often,' he laughed. 'But we made it, that's the key thing, and this flight is only a couple of hours, then we'll be safely in Florence. Nothing else can go wrong now.' She pulled a face at him and crossed herself. 'Don't bring the evil eye on us!' she said with a laugh and they turned to watch the safety procedure routine of the bored-looking stewardesses.

☼

Despite Adam's evocation tempting the Gods of travel, the flight ran smoothly, and they landed at Peretola a few minutes ahead of schedule, Adam and Sofia positively sauntering through to the baggage claims hall, relaxed in the knowledge they had arrived at their destination. An hour later, when the carousel was empty bar one abandoned suitcase, its jaunty red ribbon tied to the handle, flapping desolately with each circuit, they admitted defeat.

Wearily, Adam rose to his feet with a sigh. 'Come on, Sofia, they're obviously not here. Let's go over to the desk to report them missing.' It hadn't occurred to either of them that as they had barely made the connection, their luggage would have stood no chance of making it. The bubbly lady behind the desk, who waved away their despair with a flick of her hand, confirmed this. 'Do not worry,' she said, looking at them brightly, 'your bags are still at Schiphol, but there are more flights coming today. They will get here later and we will bring them to your hotel.'

They finished filling in the PIR forms, then made their way dejectedly through passport control and into the outside world. The warmth and sunlight that greeted them took Sofia's breath away. Then it dawned on her, she was in Italy. A huge smile spread across her face as the excited chatter of passers-by registered, and she had a sense of coming home. Adam was sullenly scrolling through his phone, looking at the emails that had come in whilst he'd been offline. She tugged on his arm. 'Come on, Adam, cheer up. We are here; our bags will join us later. Let's get to the hotel and start checking out Florence!'

Her excitement rubbed off on him, so he smiled. Putting away his phone, he pointed over to the taxi rank 'OK, we can grab a taxi to the hotel and get checked in.'

Easing into the back seat, Sofia let forth a babble of Italian which the driver acknowledged with a gruff, 'Sì, *signora*,' then they were off. Everything Adam had heard about driving in Italy was true. The fifteen-minute drive into the centre was terrifying, and he feared for his life the entire way. Sofia seemed oblivious, gazing rapturously out of the window and pointing out everything that caught her attention. When the car screeched to a halt outside of their hotel, he let go of his hold on the strap, his fingers cramping from the strain. Determined to take control back, he strode ahead into the hotel and up to the reception desk.

The man behind the desk, who looked like a young De Niro, was looking at his computer screen and didn't even look up when Adam said 'Good Morning.' Holding an imperious finger in the air to show he should wait, the clerk continued with whatever held his attention. Adam felt his hackles rise but counted to ten, refusing to lose his cool in front of Sofia again. When the man, whose name badge declared him to be Guido, finally looked up, he smiled charmingly and said 'how may I help you, Sir?' in exceptionally good English.

'Two rooms under the names Flynn and Marino?' he replied, returning the smile, thankful he hadn't started shouting for attention.

Guido looked back at his computer, a frown appearing as he scrolled up and down. 'Are you sure it was for today?' he asked, looking at Adam inquisitively. Adam felt an ice-cold sensation slide through his body. 'Yes, of course, I'm sure. Adam Flynn and Sofia Marino from Sublime Retreats, two rooms starting today for two weeks,' he responded, trying to keep his voice even. Sofia sidled up to him. 'What's up?'

'I'm sure it's fine,' he replied, not looking at her 'just having trouble finding the booking.'

'Aha,' announced Guido 'I see.'

Relief washed over Adam and he felt slightly sick 'so you've found the booking?'

'I have found the email we sent requesting confirmation, Mr Flynn, but I am not finding a response.'

With a sinking feeling, Adam realised his worst nightmare was coming true. He had forgotten something, all that careful planning and meticulous attention to detail blown out of the water with one silly moment. He could remember it, the email coming in; him filing it away, mentally marked to be done later. But he hadn't, had he, he'd left it sitting there, and now they were here with no hotel booked. He felt his control slipping.

'OK,' he said evenly, 'we'd like two rooms for two weeks please, Guido,' and gave him his most confident smile.

'I'm sorry, *Signore*, we are fully booked. The entire city is, it's August!'

Adam thought he was going to faint. The long flight, the mad dash and the helter-skelter like taxi ride had taken their toll. He felt light-headed and sank on the sofa to the right of the reception desk. Seeing his pallor and dumbstruck expression, Sofia stepped in to help. She smiled sweetly at Guido and asked quickly, in Italian, if he had any availability at all. A brief conversation later, he was handing her a key, all smiles and best wishes. Sofia walked over and looked down at Adam.

'Right, we have a room, just one mind you, and just for tonight, but it's a start,' she said brightly. When he didn't respond she said 'are you OK?'

'Of course I am not bloody OK,' he growled, his eyes flashing with frustration. 'I ballsed things up, the whole trip in jeopardy because I missed something.' He looked down at his hands on his lap, lost in the turmoil of regret.

'Pull yourself together, man,' Sofia snapped. 'We have a room for now. Our bags will be here later and we can sort out another place to stay for tomorrow. It's not the end of the world!'

Pulling his mind out from the self-pitying loop it and fallen into, he stood. 'You are right, of course. Sorry Sofia, but you know how much work I've put into this. I can't believe I forgot something so basic.'

'We all make mistakes, Adam, don't be so hard on yourself,' she said, rubbing his arm. 'Come on, our room is on the first floor. Let's go dump our stuff and then have a look round. My stomach tells me it's lunchtime.'

The small twin room was at the back of the hotel, offering a view of the wall of the next building. But it was clean and available, so neither of them minded too much. The cramped space meant they had to shuffle past each other to get to the bathroom. While Adam freshened up, Sofia sat on her bed, connected to the Wi-Fi and looked at Margarita's Instagram feed. The pictures brought a smile to her face and a tear to her eye.

The party had obviously been an enormous success and run into the night with endless shots of happy, smiling, slightly glassy-eyed groups enjoying themselves. She looked closer at the last picture. In the background she could see Suzie and Aldo sitting, heads together, on a chair, deep in conversation, smiling at each other. 'About bloody time,' she said and was about to put the phone down when a long-winded message came through from her ma, reminding her to call Uncle Joey. As Adam was showing no signs of coming out and she could still hear water splashing, she dialled the number and waited for her uncle to answer.

'*Ciao, Zio*,' she smiled down the phone at the sound of his gravelly voice.

'*Tesoro*, Sofia!' he exclaimed. 'It is so good to hear your voice, it's been too long. Tell me, are you here, did your flight get in OK?'

'Yes Zio, not without mishap but I'm here,' she laughed 'but I can tell you all about it when I see you. Listen, you may be able to help.' She said and explained the situation with the hotel, or lack of one.

'*Si, si posso aiutare*. Of course I can help; you can stay at my apartment in the palazzo. I'm not using it at the moment. Stay as long as you need,' he said generously.

'Oh, that would be fantastic,' she said, turning to give Adam a thumbs up as he emerged from the bathroom. 'I will call you for details tomorrow and we can arrange to meet. *Grazie per l'aiuto, sei un angelo.*'

Looking at Adam excitedly, she said, 'I have somewhere for us to stay! My Uncle has a place here; he said we can use that. Isn't that just perfect?'

Adam, who'd been hiding in the bathroom with the taps running, Googling hotels and finding nothing that would work, felt relieved. He would much rather he had found a solution, but ultimately he was just happy that it solved the problem. He frowned 'you have family here? I thought they were from Sicily?'

'Oh we are, but my family gets everywhere,' she giggled, bouncing off the bed and towards the bathroom. 'Two minutes and I'm with you,' she called as she shut the door.

Adam sank onto his bed, a feeling of unease creeping through him. It seemed odd that he was now accepting help from the family he and his pop were so sure were criminals. It didn't sit well, but currently, he didn't see what else he could do.

PRENDI IL TUO PARTNER PER LA GOLA

(Take your partner by the throat)

A s they made their way through the lobby and past the reception, Guido called out, 'Signora! Signora Marino!' and Sofia turned and walked up to the desk. 'Ciao, Guido, what's up?'

'I have spoken with the manager, and although of course this unfortunate situation is in no way our fault, we would like to offer you both a complimentary meal in our rooftop terrace restaurant as a gesture of goodwill.'

'That would be wonderful!' she said, turning to Adam with a radiant smile. 'Isn't that great?' she asked him. Adam didn't really want reminding of this "unfortunate situation" but couldn't fault their level of customer service.

'That's very gracious of you,' he said to Guido, 'if we could reserve a table for say, 7 pm?'

'*Si, si signor*,' the receptionist replied and with a couple of strokes on the keyboard, confirmed their booking for that night. Sofia, who had picked up one of the complimentary maps on the counter, squealed excitedly. 'Adam, we're just a short walk from Ponte Vecchio. Can we go there first? Please?' she implored.

'Sure,' he replied with an avuncular smile, 'it's as good a place to start as any.'

Out in the intense heat on the street, as they made their way towards the famous bridge, he watched her. Sofia was spinning around in the manner of Julie Andrews on top of her mountain, in her effort to take everything in. Her head craned upwards, pointing out various landmarks. She was repeatedly bumping into people and their passage left echoes of '*Scuzi*' in its wake as she bounded on to the next sighting. "It's like taking a puppy for a walk," he smiled to himself, but let her continue to lead him exuberantly down the small streets.

She picked up speed when she spotted the muddy waters of the Arno and pulled him deeper into the cobbled street that led to the bridge, pushing through the throngs of tourists perusing the beautiful shops that lined the way. She stopped suddenly outside a jewellery shop, eyes captured by the bright baubles in the window. Pressing her nose up to the glass, she was admiring a tray of silver charms greedily and called to him, 'come here, Adam, look at these. My pa said I should collect charms from my travels.' Coming to stand beside her, he glanced at the wares on offer. 'That's a really neat idea,' he said, 'but don't you think you should wait? See what's available before rushing in to buy something from the first place you see?'

'God! Are you always this cautious?' she demanded, and marched determinedly into the store, leaving him feeling slightly lacking on the pavement. He watched the purchase play out through the window, her shining enthusiasm bringing out smiles of joy in the tiny Geppetto-like shopkeeper who rushed to show her the tray of charms she was pointing to. He saw her fluttering with indecision between two of the tiny ornaments, going from one to the other, unable to leave one behind. "Geppetto" then said something which caused her to unleash her wonderful smile and lean over the counter, kissing him on both cheeks, bringing a rosy glow to them. "Well, I'll be dammed," he thought to himself "he's just given her one for free, I'm sure of it!" Shaking his head in amazement, he watched the final act of the purchase, much gesticulation and salutations in true Italian fashion, before she emerged back onto the street clutching her purchases.

Grinning triumphantly at him, she waved the bag in his face. 'All done, come on. We need to get some shots of you on the bridge; it will make a great post for your feed!'

He had to admit that it was a beautiful place, the muted tones of ancient stonework, the brightly lit windows of tiny, Victorian-looking shops. He felt a sense of the history here, something you didn't get back home, where everything was bright, shiny and new. They paused by the archways in the centre of the bridge, waiting their turn while the other tourists took their pictures, before Sofia thrust him to the wall and said 'stand there' while pulling her phone out.

She took a few snaps, then paused, lowering the phone to look at him. 'Could you at least smile, Adam? Look like you're happy to be here?' He grinned spontaneously, and she caught it. Looking happily at the screen she said 'that's the one, you should smile more often you know.' Unsure how to reply to that, he just stood looking at her quizzically. 'Anyway, let's go find somewhere to eat, I'm famished,' she said and walked back the way they had come.

'How about there?' he said to her, pointing to a place as they meandered up the street. She looked where he was pointing, a small stylish café declaring it had fresh juices and organic produce.

'No way, mister,' she said decisively, 'we are in Italy and you are going to eat some actual food for once' and she pulled him towards some outside tables at a restaurant called Trattoria Napoleone. She was soon drooling over the menu, indecision flaring up again. 'Oh my God, this all sounds amazing,' she said, looking up and noticing Adam had put the menu back on the table. 'Why aren't you looking?' she asked, taking a sip of water from the glass the waiter had brought for them.

'It's in Italian, Sofia, I have no idea, apart from a few words, what it's saying,' he said sheepishly, feeling uncomfortably out of place and no longer in control. Seeing his discomfort she said, 'OK, well why don't I order a few things for us to share? '

'You mean like Tapas?'

She laughed, 'yes, like Tapas, Adam, but we're in Italy, so it's antipasti.'

It wasn't long before the waiter was bringing what seemed like a never-ending stream of dishes. As he placed each one on the table, she leaned in and inhaled, closing her eyes in ecstasy and letting out a small moan that had Adam shifting in his seat.

'So,' he said, looking at the plates suspiciously, 'what do we have? I recognise, of course, the plates of meats and cheeses. But what's this?' he said, prodding at a dish with his knife. She was pouring him a glass of ruby red Chianti and looked over her pouring arm to see what he was asking about.

'Ah,' she said, placing the bottle carefully back on the table 'that is *polentine fritta con pate de fegato e funghi porcini*' and laughed openly at his bemused expression. 'Just try it, Adam, live a little,' she said with a smile, helping herself to a large portion. He tentatively took a piece and placed it on his plate, looking at it like it might crawl away any second. She watched intently as he cut a small forkful and brought it slowly to his mouth. He chewed experimentally for a moment before breaking out into a smile of wonderment, which thrilled her to the core.

Adam felt like his taste buds were exploding with joy, years of denial making it so much more intense. He shovelled in another forkful, chewing away happily, and pointed to another dish 'and that?' She noticed he didn't wait to hear her answer but helped himself to a liberal portion without pausing. She knew she had gone some way towards breaking through his uptight shield.

'They are *coccolifritti*, very typical of the area. But as I said, just give it a try, Adam; it's the only way to experience Italy.'

When Adam finally laid his cutlery down in defeat, it amazed him to see they had pretty much cleared the table. He could not remember the last time he had enjoyed a meal so much or felt this full. Leaning back in his chair, stretching his stomach to make room, he patted it contentedly. He'd lost the battle with his strict healthy eating mandate after the first bite and consoled his guilt with the fact that he was abroad. It didn't count, and he had to experience what the club members were going to have when they got here. Happy with his excuses he said, 'I'm not sure we're going to need dinner tonight after all that.'

'You'd be surprised,' she said knowingly, smiling up at the waiter, who was placing the bill on the table along with two glasses of complimentary grappa. 'Drink that,' she nodded at the glass in front of him 'it will help your meal go down' and took a sip from her glass. The cool, aromatic liquid slipped down easily, despite how full he felt. It was quite refreshing.

They sat enjoying the sunshine, chatting away easily about their day tomorrow, the first of the hectic schedule. Realising they had been there for some time, Adam said 'we should move really, we're keeping the table.'

'It's not a problem, Adam. I mean we can go if you want, but the staff won't mind, this is normal here,' she said, waving her hand to encompass the dining area and he could see that she was right. Many of the tables were devoid of food and the diners were relaxing, talking amiably and the staff were not in the least bit concerned. It was quite liberating after the hustle and bustle of Houston, where everything happened so fast.

☼

They decided to walk off their meal a little before going back to the hotel and wandered happily through the streets with no particular agenda. When they entered Piazza del Duomo, they both stopped in their tracks, looking up at the building in awe. With the dazzling colours reflecting the afternoon sunlight, the towering bronze doors and its distinguishable dome were all things they had seen in photographs many times, but they had not done them justice.

'That is awesome,' said Adam, echoing Sofia's thought, 'shall we go inside?'

'We should wait,' she turned to answer him, 'it is part of one of the tours I want us to try.'

'Makes sense,' he said, looking around, trying to take everything in. Sofia suddenly grabbed his hand and pulled him over to a shopfront to their left with a queue lining up to get through the door. He saw customers coming out, happily licking gaily coloured balls of ice cream, nestled in cones and covered with sauce.

'Really? You think we need more food?' he couldn't help but laugh.

'It's Gelato, it doesn't count,' she grinned. 'Anyway, their sign says they are the first organic gelato company, so you have to try.'

He had to admit the creamy gelato with hazelnuts and chocolate that he chose was out of this world; he made a note of the name EdoardoIl Gelato Biologico, to add to his info file.

'Look, they're on Instagram,' she said, pointing up to a sign with her cone, which had #EDOARDOGELATO in bold letters at the bottom. 'We should take some pictures and tag them in it. It will add more traction to your feed.'

'You may as well be speaking Italian again, I hear those words but it means nothing to me.'

'Don't worry; I know what I'm doing. Let's finish these and find somewhere with Wi-Fi to have a coffee, then we can get you set up. The next few days are going to be hectic but full of opportunities for wonderful pictures.' Sofia soon had him posing again, in front of the doors to the Duomo, encouraging him to expressively lick his gelato in a way that made him feel very uncomfortable. He wasn't sure he was cut out to be a model.

They managed to get a seat outside L'Opera Caffè by dint of Sofia nimbly darting through the throng and nabbing a table that was just becoming available. He followed, ignoring the glares of other tourists patiently waiting to be seated. As she confidently ordered their drinks from a very attentive server, who seemed to be charming her judging by her giggles and tossing of hair, he felt another flash of heat in his stomach, and he recognised it as anger. Jealousy to be exact.

Sofia spent the next hour setting up his Instagram account and trying to explain it to him. He felt like a dinosaur as she flicked through his phone, following certain accounts, adding photos and, apparently, hashtags. 'There you go,' she said finally, handing it back to him 'you're all set up. We just have to make sure we add things every day, the trick is to be consistent.' Taking the device from her, he looked pointlessly at the app, deciding he would Google the idiot's 'how to' later so she wouldn't think he was completely stupid. He noticed it was nearly five o'clock and was amazed. Where had the afternoon gone?

He looked over; Sofia was nibbling the biscuit that had come with her coffee, looking down at her phone with complete concentration. A strand of hair had fallen forward, and he resisted the urge to reach over and tuck it behind her ear. Alarmed at this surge of what he could only call affection, he made busy with his phone and checked his emails.

From: Peterwilliams@sublimeretreats.com

To: Adamflynn@sublimeretreats.com

Subject: Italy Product Trip

Good morning Adam,

I just wanted to check in and make sure all is going well and that you and Sofia have arrived safely in Italy.

I appreciate you have a busy few days ahead but please keep me up to date.

Marc is coming home today. I have arranged for someone to care for him here, so I will be able to spend some time in the office next week.

Best regards,

Peter

General Manager - Sublime Retreats

Adam felt immediately contrite. He should have emailed Peter before when they had arrived, but with the disaster of the hotel booking and the distraction of, well, of Sofia, he hadn't. He quickly typed out a response, assuring Peter that all was well and he would indeed keep him updated. A thought occurred, and he emailed Tim and proudly told him about his new 'Insta' account. Adam picked up the bill and pulled out some notes to pay, looking around to attract a server's attention.

'Just leave it on the table,' said Sofia, standing up with a stretch that pulled her t-shirt firmly over her pert breasts. He looked away quickly, placing the money on the table. It felt very weird just leaving it there and walking away, like they were leaving without paying. Italy was certainly very different from everything he knew and was going to take some getting used to.

☼

Back in the hotel room, it was a little awkward. Squeezing past each other to gain access to the bathroom wasn't ideal, and Sofia felt very self-conscious when she went in to take a shower. She looked back at Adam who was perched on his bed with his laptop, absorbed in what he could see on the glowing screen and told herself not to be silly. Closing the door, she gratefully stripped off her clothes, standing under the shower with relief. It had been a long, hot, tiring day - she felt grimy.

Her thoughts wandered to Adam as she soaped herself, remembering his look of pure joy when he tasted the food, his obvious enjoyment of the gelato. She had noticed his eyes drawn to her breasts when she had stretched at the café. The thought of him looking at her now sent a frisson of lust through her. Despite being alone, she blushed at the compelling urge to touch herself, turning the water fully to the right onto the coldest setting, trying to freeze away her feelings under the icy jets.

Adam was having similar issues. Knowing she was in there naked was driving him nuts. He had to force visions of her soapy body out of his head while he tried to concentrate on work. It relieved him to see she was fully dressed when she emerged. If she had just had a towel wrapped around her, he wasn't sure he could resist the temptation to pluck it away and watch it slip to the floor, revealing what he could so easily imagine was hidden beneath.

She seemed a little distant now, a little cold. All her joie de vivre seemed to have seeped away in the shower. He wasn't sure why, but it made things easier on him as they got ready in such proximity to go up to the roof terrace for dinner. Sofia stood in front of the full-length mirror on the back of the door, brushing out her hair, happy with the little orange summer dress and strappy sandals she had chosen to wear. He watched her out of the corner of his eye; she looked gorgeous. The dress she was wearing hugged her body and skimmed her thighs in all the right ways.

'You look great,' he called over to her, and their eyes met in the mirror for a long moment.

'Thanks,' she replied, breaking the moment. 'You don't look too bad yourself.' Despite the heat of the city, he had on well-fitting jeans and a blue t-shirt which she was pretty sure matched the colour of his eyes behind those glasses. 'Come on, there's a free dinner waiting for us upstairs.'

LE CONVERSAZIONI INTIME

(Intimate conversations)

They took the lift to the fifth floor where they were greeted by a haughty looking maître d' who, once he'd confirmed their reservation, led them gracefully out to the terrace and a candle-lit table set for two.

'Oh, my,' Sofia said, hand fluttering to her mouth as she took in the spectacular panoramic view of the Florentine skyline, hues of indigo running to rose gold where the sun was setting. She walked up to the railing and stretched out her hand, Brunelleschi's Dome and Giotto's Tower appearing close enough to touch. She turned to Adam, a look of wonder on her face. 'This is definitely somewhere we have to recommend to members.'

He nodded. It was stunning by any standards. He couldn't imagine a more perfect or more romantic view. Noticing the maître d' passively standing by the table, waiting to seat them, Sofia dragged herself away and uttered her thanks as he held out her chair. Once she was seated, he picked up her napkin, opening it with an expert flick of his wrist, letting it float down to settle on her lap. He left, assuring them that a server would be with them shortly, leaving a silence in his wake. Apart from the clinking of cutlery and the low, muted conversation from the few other diners that were there, their table was blanketed in a suppressed atmosphere of expectation.

They both looked around, pretending to be absorbed in the view, occasionally catching each other's eye and grinning but unable to think of a word to say. The air was thick between them, and neither knew how to break its spell.

The welcome arrival of the server with the menus provided a starting point for a conversation, allowing them to ignore the strange pressure that was building between them. After a brief discussion, they opted to follow the waiter's advice and order the Tuscan Traditional Dishes set menu, as well as his recommendation for the best wine to accompany their meal. Spell broken, they fell into simple conversation, reclaiming some of the easy banter from earlier that day. They chatted briefly about the first appointment early tomorrow, Sofia checking the location on her phone and confirming it was an easy ten-minute walk away.

The waiter returned, pouring a measure of wine for Adam to taste before filling their glasses after his nod of approval. 'My, this place is fancy,' said Sofia, taking her first sip with obvious enjoyment. 'Couldn't be further from Margarita's, despite them both being Italian,' she laughed, feeling a sudden pang for her home. Seeing her wistful gaze Adam asked, 'so what's it like?' and she happily chattered about the restaurant that her family had run for so many years, pulling out her phone to show him the pictures of the party and her family.

Despite the happy, smiling faces of her brothers, Adam couldn't help but think they looked a bit menacing, reminding him of his father's words of warning and the fact that tomorrow they would move to her uncle's apartment. He was extremely unhappy with the arrangement, but what could he do? He had looked online again today, but there was nowhere in a central location that had availability for the full duration of their stay. Just random nights here and there, and they couldn't afford to waste the time flitting from one place to the next with the schedule they had. His hands were tied, but he had decided to call his pop and ask him if he could find any information about this 'Uncle Joey,' see what he was getting himself into.

The first course arrived, fennel infused *Finocchiona* salami with crostini, and it surprised him to find that he was hungry again, devouring it with gusto. The Ravioli that followed was unlike any he'd had before, and with further amazement he tucked into the perfectly cooked beef sirloin with an exquisite Chianti sauce that soon followed, matching Sofia's appetite bite for bite. When the quintessential Tiramisù was placed in front of him, he already felt stuffed but attempted a few mouthfuls. Why not? He was in Italy and should enjoy everything it offered. He looked at Sofia speculatively as she licked the last of her dessert from her spoon.

'Everything to your satisfaction, signore?' said the maître d' who'd appeared unnoticed on silent feet next to him. Startled from his reverie, Adam said enthusiastically, 'Yes, splendid. The entire meal was fantastic.' Sofia smiled to herself. Watching him enjoy his food without a second thought had been almost as enjoyable as eating it herself. She held up her phone, asking the maître d' 'would you take a picture of us?'

Looking taken aback, but seemingly unable to resist Sofia any more than anyone else, he complied, waving them closer together with his hand as he focused the camera. Breathing in the heady smell of jasmine as she leaned into him, Adam felt contentment he couldn't recall feeling for years, not since he was a child, at least. His smile that was captured in the photo was beaming, nearly as radiant as hers.

☼

Back in their room, the awkward waltz in the cramped space resumed as they both got ready for bed. With the lights off, they lay there, unable to sleep, hyperaware of the presence in the next bed. After a while, just as she was drifting off, she heard Adam say, 'I really enjoyed today, Sofia, thank you.' When slumber finally took her away, it was with a gentle smile on her lips.

The ululation of their dual alarms dragged them both from a deep sleep the next morning. Adam stretched out, not wanting to leave the cocoon of warmth and the memory of the dreams he had. Sofia, however, leapt up, excited to start another day. Looking at herself in the mirror as she brushed her teeth, she made a note to call her uncle this morning to sort out the apartment. But first, coffee!

'Come on, sleepyhead,' she called to the supine form of Adam, who didn't seem to have moved, nudging him as she walked past. Begrudgingly, he sat up, wiping sleepy eyes before patting the bedside table with a splayed hand until he located his glasses. He flicked them open with one hand and put them on, looking at her grumpily. 'Are you always this damn chipper in the mornings?'

'Pretty much,' she replied extra chirpily, laughing as he winced. 'Up you get, Adam, we've got a lot to do today.'

Breakfast was being served on the same terrace as dinner last night, the atmosphere completely different in the bright morning light but the view still as remarkable. Sitting under a large white umbrella, shading them from the glare, Sofia sipped on her first coffee of the day, munching between sips on a croissant while Adam assuaged his guilt with some fruit salad and a mixed juice.

Answering her phone with a smile, Sofia said 'Buongiorno Zio' and had a rapid-fire conversation with a deep-voiced man that Adam felt sure must be her uncle. When the call ended she explained, 'that was my Uncle Joey, about the apartment? It's all arranged; he's going to text me the address.' Her phone chimed to confirm this. Looking at the message, she checked the location. 'Oh, it's perfect, Adam, on the banks of the Arno, close to here!' Chewing on the last bite of her pastry she added 'it's over a restaurant, we can pick up the keys from there he said.'

It seemed like there was nothing he could add to this, so he just nodded, thinking they could leave their luggage at the reception and collect them later, after their viewings today. Back in their room, packing didn't take long after just one night and they deposited the bags with Guido for safekeeping before going to meet the property agent outside the first apartment.

Andrea Ferrari was as sleek as his namesake, with his slicked-back hair, trimmed goatee and an extremely well-cut suit. He swooped in on Sofia as soon as they made introductions. Adam felt a twinge of anger at the attention being lavished on her, and an intense dislike for his insidious charm. It relieved him when they entered the cool, dim courtyard of the Palazzo; the heat was already getting to him, even though it was still early in the day. He noticed Andrea looked perfectly at ease, giving off an air of coolness, despite the three-piece suit he was wearing.

The inner courtyard, so typical of Florentine architecture, was peaceful, the closing of the large panelled door seeming to block out the outside world completely. As they made their way up the staircase to the top floor, Andrea told them a little about the area and the benefits of the apartment they were going to see. The apartment was beautiful, with huge vaulted ceilinged rooms yet modern fixtures and fittings. It was a good start to their search, Adam thought, although it wasn't quite the right one. The agent had obviously taken on board his requirements; it boded well for them to find something.

And so the day progressed as they went to see the other three apartments, Adam traipsing wearily behind Sofia and Andrea, chattering between themselves punctuated with her peals of laughter. When they stopped for lunch Adam was glad to sit down in the shade, his body clock telling him he should still be asleep right now. When Andrea excused himself to go to the bathroom, Sofia took the opportunity to ask, 'so, what do you think of what we've seen so far?'

Adam considered the three that they had seen 'they are all remarkable properties, but nothing is leaping at me yet as being the one,' he said, making speech marks with his fingers. 'Let's see what the last one today offers, then we can talk through them later. Do me a favour, I appreciate you're in Italy, but please remember I don't speak Italian. It's a little rude of you and him to exclude me.' He jerked his thumb toward the approaching agent, a sneer on his face.

Crestfallen, Sofia nodded and pointedly spoke to Andrea in English for the rest of the time, even when he spoke Italian to her. If he found something strange in that, he didn't show it, and he remained charmed by everything she said. When the agent left them after the last appointment, he spent far too long kissing her goodbye as far as Adam was concerned, but aware that he had upset Sofia with his earlier comment, kept his thoughts to himself as they went back to the hotel to collect their bags.

Despite his desire to never enter an Italian taxi again, his desire not to walk another step that day won out and Adam asked the ever-present Guido to summon them a ride. They were feeling the effects of jetlag now, wilting in the heat and looking forward to having a quiet evening in their new accommodation with the luxury of individual rooms. The short drive was over in a flash of near misses and a cacophony of blaring horns, and Adam wearily stood to one side while Sofia rapped on the door of the darkened restaurant. It was answered by a tall, young man who could easily feature on the cover of one of the glossy magazines he'd noticed in the kiosks today.

'Ciao, you must be Joey's niece,' he said in greeting, his handsome face cracking a grin that revealed perfect white teeth. 'He didn't tell me you were so beautiful!' and he leaned in to kiss her cheeks.

'For fuck's sake,' Adam muttered under his breath. The place was full of Lotharios! Pushing off the wall, he walked over to make himself known. 'Hi, I'm Adam,' he said, standing possessively next to Sofia.

'I am Stefano' replied the young Romeo, unabashed, 'wait just one moment, I will get the keys and show you up to the apartment.' He was soon bounding back through the door, easily lifting Sofia's case in one hand while opening one half of a huge, arched, dark wooden door to the side of the restaurant.

'How do you know my uncle?' Sofia asked as they climbed up yet another set of winding stairs that ran up the side of the building in the cool, filtered light of the courtyard.

'Your Uncle Joey is a good man. He owns this building. He gave me the money to start my restaurant' Stefano grinned over his shoulder at her. Adam absorbed this snippet of information for later when he could speak to his dad. Finally they reached the top floor and Stefano opened the door, standing back to let them in. Walking through the simple hallway, they were unprepared for the splendour of the palatial room it opened into. The vast space was dimly lit, the shutters of the six enormous arched windows along the outside wall closed against the afternoon sun, and just a few lamps gave off pools of light.

Stefano, coming in behind them, hit the switch on the wall, bringing the main lighting to life. Adam and Sofia wandered around in awed silence, the churchlike ambience defying them to speak. The primary room was sprawling, separated by oversized bookshelves to divide the seating and dining areas. The sky-high, heavily beamed ceiling, on closer inspection, revealed detailed engravings around each border as they climbed the curved staircase that led to the fantastic contrast of the ultra-modern kitchen on a mezzanine level, looking out over the living space, its glass-fronted balustrade protecting them from the drop.

'This place is amazing,' Sofia finally said, unable to believe she would be staying in such luxury. They returned downstairs and along the hall to inspect the bedrooms. Four in all. And a grand master suite that was spacious enough to house her entire family, she thought, as she stood gazing at the faded mural of cavorting cherubs above a bed big enough for six. The other bedrooms, although smaller, were still impressive. The walls of brushed concrete had a golden sheen that exuded luxury, and each had its own bathroom adjoining it.

Stefano, insisting that they come for dinner at the restaurant later on, once they were settled and rested, bade them a pleasant afternoon. When he had left Adam turned to Sofia 'what the hell does your uncle do? This place must be worth a fortune!'

Blowing air through pursed lips, Sofia gave a very native shrug, her face screwing up slightly as she said 'oh a little of this and that. He's what you might call an entrepreneur' she said vaguely, as she took hold of the handle of her suitcase and started trundling down the hall 'do you mind which room I take?' she called back. Still wondering what an entrepreneur could do to afford this building in the most expensive part of Florence, Adam replied, 'no preference, you can take the big one if you like.'

She'd stopped outside the room in question, looking in 'I don't think I could do it justice' she said without thinking 'that is a room for lovers.' The statement fell between them, settling into the atmosphere, an immutable idea that would lurk in corners and pop up when least expected.

Sofia shivered, turning to give him a small smile before walking down to the last room in the corridor. 'I'll take this one.' She looked at her watch. It was a little after three. 'I don't know about you but I'm going to unpack, shower, then rest for a while.'

'Sounds like a good idea,' he replied, 'let's go to dinner at about six tonight. I think we could both do with an early night.' They entered their rooms and leaned against the doors in a synchronised display of relief. Sofia pulled her case onto the luggage rack, opened it and began placing her clothes in the wardrobe, her toiletries in the bathroom. She couldn't believe she'd said that room was for lovers! What an idiot she was. Her toes curled in embarrassment. She really should think before opening her mouth, especially around Adam, of all people. Trying not to think about it, she flopped onto her bed with her phone. Counting back the hours, she knew Suzie should be up by now and sent her a message. She felt the need to touch base with something or someone familiar.

Sure enough, a few minutes later a string of emojis popped up on her screen and they chatted back and forth for a while before Suzie had to leave for work. Sofia was dying to ask her if anything had happened with Aldo, but that was a conversation that needed to happen face to face. Forgetting she had planned to have a shower, she drew up the blanket and sank further into the downy pillows and was soon fast asleep.

☼

Adam, however, showered before he did anything else. A day of sweating and discomfort, trekking around the city, however beautiful, had left him drained. He gazed around his room, taking in the quality of the fixtures and fittings with a practised eye, as he dialled his pop's number.

'So, you're still alive, Son?' Jack answered, sounding sleepy.

'Sorry, Pop, did I wake you?' asked Adam, double-checking the time difference in his mind.

'No worries, I was just about to get up anyways. How are things going with the trip, the Marino girl giving you any cause for concern?'

A scramble of images flashed across Adam's mind, Sofia laughing, teasing him, the thought of her lithe body naked in the shower. 'No, I don't think we have anything to worry about with her, to be honest,' he said, 'but I would like you to check someone out for me.' He explained to Jack about the mysterious Uncle Joey, his largesse with the young man in the restaurant downstairs and the splendour of this apartment, one of who knew how many in this building.

'Sounds interesting, and she wouldn't say what he does?' he

asked when Adam finished.

'Nope. She was pretty reticent about it.'

'OK, leave it with me. Let me make a couple of calls and see what I can find out. I'll be in touch.'

Adam wasn't entirely convinced with his dad's theory about the Marino family, but at least it gave his old man something to do.

IL BRIVIDO DELLA CACCIA

(The thrill of the chase)

From: Adamflynn@sublimeretreats.com

To: Peterwilliams@sublimeretreats.com

Subject: Italy Product Trip

Good morning Peter,

I hope all is well, and Marc is recovering at a good rate?

Our first day of viewings went well; it seems the agent has a good understanding of our requirements. Although I feel none of the four apartments we saw today was the ideal property for us, I am hopeful that we will find the perfect one for City Breaks in the next few days.

As a side note, I'd just like to say you were justified in choosing Sofia for this trip. She has proved resourceful and has been a real asset.

I will report back tomorrow after the next round of viewings.

Best regards,

Adam

After a moment's hesitation, Adam hit the send button. He wasn't completely comfortable that he hadn't mentioned the mess up with the hotel and their current accommodation. But he thought it might sound less important when they were back, flagship apartment signed, trip successful. Mentioning Sofia's contributions to the trip went some way to salve his guilt at the rummaging around in her family's history that was currently going on back in Houston. And he had to admit, so far, she had proved indispensable. As annoying as that was, he knew he would have floundered without her wits and charm.

Lying on the luxurious double bed, he let his thoughts wander over the events of the last 24 hours. It certainly hadn't been the smooth plain sailing that he had envisaged, but they had got through it, he thought with a wry smile, as sleep stole up and took him away. When he surfaced, he found Sofia up in the kitchen, the smell of coffee giving her location away. She looked up as he reached the top of the stairs and gave him a welcoming smile.

'Hi, Adam, did you manage to get some sleep?' she asked as she stirred her drink.

'Yes I did, still feel pretty exhausted really but I think a good night's sleep tonight will set me straight.' He opened the fridge, relieved to see there were some small bottles of water in there. He took one out and drained it in one long gulp. 'We'll have to get some supplies in,' he said, crumpling the bottle and placing it in the container marked for recycling.

'We can do that tomorrow, we've got dinner downstairs tonight and we can grab breakfast on the way to meet Andrea in the morning'. At the mention of the agent's name, his face formed a pout, a little moue of distaste.

'You don't like him much, do ya?' she asked with a grin.

'I just find his fawning over you a little unprofessional,' he said, trying and failing to sound casual.

They stared at each other for a long moment until a chiming from his phone broke the spell. Looking down, he saw it was a response from Peter. Skimming the brief reply he said to her, 'it's Peter, wishing us well for tomorrow. I sent him a report about today's viewings.'

'It's a shame none of them ticked all the boxes,' she said, finishing her coffee and rinsing the cup out. She stopped suddenly, whirling around with an excited look on her face 'What about this place?' she asked enthusiastically.

Adam blanched. The same thought had occurred to him earlier, but there was no way he was doing business with 'Uncle Joey' and he had already come up with a failing. 'No outside space' he shrugged as if it disappointed him. Her face fell, 'oh yes, I didn't think of that. It's such a shame, everything else is perfect!'

Not wanting to talk about the possibilities of the apartment anymore, Adam, looking at the time, said 'shall we go down for dinner?'

'Sure, let me just run a brush through my hair and grab my phone and I'll be with you,' she replied, before running lightly down the steps.

☼

The restaurant, having just opened, was empty. Stefano rushed forward with his playboy smile to greet them 'where would you like to sit?' he asked, waving his hand around the empty tables 'We rarely get people in this early' he grinned. They chose a small table in the corner by the window so they could watch the people pass by as they discussed the apartments they'd seen and the hopefuls lined up for tomorrow. Stefano returned with the menus and a carafe of red wine. 'This is from my family's vineyard in Umbria,' he said proudly, pouring them both a glass and standing back expectantly. Dutifully, they picked them up, Adam sniffing it ostentatiously before they both took a sip.

'Wow, that's amazing,' said Sofia with her usual gusto, taking another greedy sip. Adam had to agree it was wonderful, full-bodied with a fruity finish, 'it's good' he grudgingly admitted. Satisfied, Stefano left them to look over the menus, and Adam was relieved to see there were English translations. Having to rely on Sofia to choose his food all the time was making him feel emasculated. Sofia found she was drawn unexpectedly to the pizzas on the list; the sight of the traditional oven behind the counter had made her long for her family. She had been determined to eat everything except pizza on this trip but allowed herself a small comfort of home, ordering the ultra-spicy Diablo. Adam selected the Bisteccheo alla Palermitana, a Palermo Style grilled rib-eye steak which sounded interesting. When it came, the perfectly cooked meat was topped with a salty, crunchy mixture of garlicky capers over a bed of wine broiled tomatoes.

The meal was a relaxed affair, with none of the formality of the previous evening, both of them feeling more at home in the laid-back atmosphere of this restaurant, making it even more enjoyable. Their conversation meandered easily beyond work and on to a more personal level, growing up, their families, and ending with a discussion of favourite films as Stefano cleared away their plates and asked if they would like dessert.

'I'm not sure I can manage it,' Sofia said shamefacedly 'we've eaten so much this last couple of days, I believe I will have to go shopping for new clothes if we carry on at this rate!' Laughing at her admission, Adam agreed but nodded when Stefano declared he would bring an *Amaro* to wash down their food. When he came back with the bittersweet smelling liquid he said, 'why don't you take them up to the roof terrace, enjoy it while watching the city skyline?'

'There's a terrace?' Sofia queried, eyes lighting up at the thought.

'Yes, sorry, I should have said. Just beyond the door to your apartment, you will see another, smaller door. Just go through there, up the stairs and you can look at the stars.'

Following his directions, they carefully carried their glasses upstairs, through the last door in the passage. A short flight of steps topped with another door, once opened, revealed a terrace that encompassed the whole of the building. It was draped in twinkling fairy lights that hung in loops around the walls and the pergola at the far side had a table and chairs conveniently placed underneath it to enjoy the view. Placing her glass on the table, Sofia stepped over to the wall, looking around at the city lit up around them, the Ponte Vecchio visible in the distance and the low hum of boats traversing the Arno floating up to them. Turning and walking back to join Adam where he sat at the table, quietly sipping his drink and enjoying the night air, she looked down at him and said 'Well?'

Taken aback, Adam looked up 'Well, what?'

'Doesn't this now make this the most perfect apartment for Sublime Retreats?' she insisted. Adam shifted in his seat. She was right, of course. This terrace ticked the last box on his list.

'You may have a point,' he said eventually, unable to deny its attractions, 'but we have to keep to the plan, see the rest. Besides, your uncle is probably not interested in renting this out to us. I'm sure he likes to use it for himself.' He ended with what he felt was a compelling reason.

'You never know until you ask,' she declared huffily, finishing her drink and thumping the glass on the table. She was sure that it was just his usual annoying cautiousness coming into play.

Adam stood up and moved next to her, his closeness confusingly making her want to lean into him and feel his arms around her and run away as fast as possible at the same time.

'Sofia, I don't dispute what you are saying. I'm just aware there are other choices, some that may be even better, and we should see them before making any decisions. This isn't like the charms for your bracelet, where you can just rush in and buy the first things that catch your eye,' he tried to joke.

Infuriated, Sofia glared up at him 'You really are insufferable,' she snapped before turning on her heels and stomping away, back through the door and down the stairs. Adam remained standing, thoughtfully finishing his Amaro, gazing out at the lights in the middle distance. He hoped to God that they would see something even more impressive tomorrow, so he could justifiably brush away her assertions that this was the perfect place. Who knew what information his dad would uncover in the next days, and he was determined not to get in any deeper with the Marino family than he already was.

The apartment was quiet when he made his way down so he sadly made his way to his room. He'd been hoping for the chance to make things right with her before he went to bed but it was obviously not to be.

☼

The next morning she greeted him with a chilly smile, her words stilted and forced. Adam hated it, he missed cheerful Sofia. He realised he'd come to enjoy her usual sunny continence; it was unbearable. As they made their way down the street in search of breakfast, she responded to his attempts at conversation with grunts and barely concealed contempt. Finally, he snapped, stopping suddenly and grabbing her by her slender shoulders. 'Sofia, please stop this. I'm sorry if I upset you,' he said, gazing down into her beautiful face.

The stream of tourists flowed around them as they remained in a tableau, gazing into each other's eyes as if searching for redemption. Overcome with an impulse he could no more ignore than he could not take his next breath, Adam leant down and gently kissed her. Tentatively at first, but as her lips responded to his, the kiss deepened, becoming something else entirely that left them gasping when they pulled apart.

The Judas' kiss revealed the attraction that they had been trying to ignore since they met. Adam reeled; he was looking down a rabbit hole, teetering on the brink of emotions strange and surreal which were waiting to entangle him. Tamping down on this Pandora's Box quickly and efficiently, unaware of hope fluttering into a corner of his consciousness, he straightened, looking at Sofia.

The sounds of the busy street re-emerged as she watched the emotions play across his face. She saw the moment, the flicker of shutters coming down in his eyes, leaving her bereft.

'A simple "sorry" would have done the trick,' she said with a brittle laugh. 'Come on, we're going to be late.'

The rest of their walk passed in silence, the kiss sitting between them, an impenetrable barrier to normal conversation. Andrea was waiting outside the coffee shop on the corner of the street that led to the first viewing of the day. He brightened at seeing them, effusively greeting them both before leading the way. Today the seemingly mindless chatter from the agent was a welcome relief to Adam. He still didn't like the man, but yesterday's irksome fawning was a Band-Aid on the mangled mess of their situation.

The first two apartments were easily dismissed, not quite having the level of opulence he was looking for, especially considering the place that they were staying he realised as he wandered around them. The third, however, pulled them both out of their fugue. White walls and pale furnishings emphasised the light that streamed in through the picture windows that displayed the view of the Arno. Tasteful artwork adorned the walls, providing points of interest as they examined each room. On the balcony, shaded from the ever bright sun, Adam's eyes sought hers. She met his glance and nodded just once, agreeing with the query in his gaze.

Picking up on their appreciation of the property, Andrea went into overdrive, extolling the virtues of the location and the asset of every feature, a caricature of the archetypical real-estate agent. Sofia caught Adam's eye, both of them grinning, amusement displacing awkwardness. After the last viewing, Andrea left them to have lunch at a trattoria run by a friend of his, jauntily walking off, confident that he was a step closer to his commission.

They faced each other over the small table in the hustle and bustle of the lunchtime rush, ignoring the stream of customers picking up their *Tramezzini* and *Pizzetta* before scurrying back to work.

'So,' said Adam, fiddling with the napkin holder on the tiny table 'about earlier…'

'There's no need to say anything, Adam, I know it meant nothing to you.'

He looked up at her phrasing. 'Did it mean something to you?' he asked, hope wafting her wings slowly, like a butterfly absorbing the sun.

Letting out a long, drawn-out breath between pursed lips, she returned his direct gaze, taking in the contours of his face, an impulse to be honest welling up. 'I think we can both admit now that we find each other attractive?' A slow blink of lids accompanied the nod that was his reply. 'But we can also both admit that this is neither the time nor the place for romance, despite' she laughed, looking around 'all this.'

The reaction of her body when he had touched his lips to hers had frightened her. The urge to drag him back to the apartment and that sumptuous bedroom for lovers had been almost overwhelming. But he was an older man, experienced; she wasn't going to admit to him her lack of familiarity in that department.

'That's sensible,' he said, falling on triteness, 'after all, we work together.'

'Exactly!' she exclaimed, a little too loudly. 'So we're agreed then. Whatever "this" is' she said, gesturing between them, 'we ignore it and get on with the job at hand?'

'Sure,' he said with a pleased smile. Giving in to that desire to kiss her had infuriated him, losing control in that simple act, going against everything he had striven for since his mother's death. Convincing himself that the matter was closed, he pointed at the menu 'what do you fancy for lunch?'

☼

Three days and twelve viewings later, they had narrowed down the options to just two potential apartments. Their relationship had slipped back a little into the previous easy-going incarnation, lacking only some of the intimacy, a resistance to touch. Sat in Stefano's restaurant that evening, they relaxed, winding down after the whirlwind of these last few days. It was Friday night, and they had decided to have the weekend off and revisit the possibles with fresh eyes on Monday.

Sated on the special of the day, *Ravioli Nudi* topped with a fresh tomato sauce and garlic-infused *Bruchetta* they accepted the second carafe of wine offered, enjoying the moment. They laughed together, over some of the jealous comments on his Instagram feed, which was full now of glorious shots of Florence, its food and its people.

'You know, I have been so busy orchestrating your social media I haven't uploaded any to mine,' Sofia said, leaning back, twirling her wine glass and watching the red liquid revolve.

'Well, we can't have that,' said Adam 'shall we take this up to the terrace? You can take some shots of that incredible view.'

Thanking Stefano for their meal and promising to return the glassware, they climbed up to the roof. The sun was setting over the Duomo, casting red streaks across the sky, and lights blinked on across the city. 'This is heavenly,' said Sofia, snapping away. Apart from that first shot of them taken by the Maître d', she had only taken a few shots of their accommodation and wanted to make sure she had memories of the city to treasure. 'Come here,' she called to Adam, let's take a selfie.'

He was so tall standing next to her; she couldn't quite get both their faces in, despite extending her arm to full length. He laughed and took the phone from her, stretching his arm and angling it so they were both in shot. The sound of the shutter resounded twice over the silent rooftop; Sofia eagerly grabbed the phone back and looked at the results. Looking up from the screen, she saw he was staring at her, something dangerous in his eyes. It felt like time stood still. Senses heightened, she could hear the distant noises of life going on below them but there was a sensation of wading through treacle as his head lowered and his lips brushed hers. He paused, looking at her, asking her permission, and her chin tilted upwards, demanding more attention from his lips.

An eternity later, she pulled back, gasping. 'Adam' her voice was raw, husky from emotion. 'I haven't… I haven't done this before.'

Momentarily confused, he looked into her sweet face, realising her meaning with a mounting astonishment that pulled him up short. Taking a step back, he explored her expression, the thrumming of his blood through his veins fighting with his conscience. 'We can stop…' he smiled gently at her. She shook her mane of hair 'that's not want I meant. I just wanted you to know.'

He stood, uncertain, all the implications of this passion chipping away at his desire. She reached up and touched his cheek 'I haven't done it before because I have never, ever felt this. What we are feeling now is…' she stopped again, her eyes pleading for understanding as her finger traced his mouth.

Lips fizzing, he took her finger and kissed it, gently nibbling, then taking it into his mouth. Sofia moaned, her head arching back, her hips pushing forward, and he knew then she was in no doubt.

They became lost, exploring each other, fierce passion throwing all caution to the wind. Sofia began tugging at his t-shirt, wanting to feel his bare skin. He complied with a swift movement and stood before her, his torso pale but firm, faint tan lines etching his biceps. She ran a slow finger from his throat, circling his chest, and then sliding lower to the trail of dark hair disappearing beneath his jeans.

Adam stood stock still, afraid to move, afraid to break the spell that had woven a gossamer thread entangling them. He grabbed her hand as it took hold of the fly on his zipper. 'Sofia,' he groaned, enflaming her further. She looked up, her eyes large pools of melted chocolate, feverish with desire. 'Are you sure?'

A slow smile spread across her face as she pulled her dress over her head, casting to one side, and stood shyly in front of him, wishing she had put on matching underwear this morning. It was his turn now to run fingers down her body, slipping under her bra and rubbing lightly over her nipples until she felt her knees give way. She leaned heavily back on the wall, eyes closed, as his other hand made its way tortuously down her belly in languid circles. Finally, brushing her through her panties, making her throw her head back, eyes wide open to the stars appearing overhead.

Shivers ran through her as he repeated the motion, again and again, waves of desire building inside her. Sofia thought she was going to explode. She looked down at his head, bent in concentration, aware that he was taking things slowly for her, feeling herself twitching inside. Delicious tremors of anticipation ebbed and flowed until she lost all control, moaning to the Florentine skies as the feelings engulfed her, finally letting out a scream the pierced the air.

He was kissing her now. As her body subsided, light butterfly kisses down her stomach and pulling her panties down to her feet. As she stepped out of them, he turned her and she gladly leant over the wall, still panting. She heard his zipper come down and felt him against her back as he undid her bra. Shrugging it off, his hands cupped her breasts and he slowly but surely entered her.

'Is it OK?' he whispered into her neck, his breath ragged, his desire blatant. Straightening her arms against the wall, she pushed back against him in answer, and as the momentum of each thrust grew, she knew she was going to come again.

Finally spent, he flopped forward onto her back, his weight pushing her into the brickwork, but she had no strength left to move. Amazed that her first time, an event she'd often daydreamed about, had been so intense, beyond anything she could have dreamt up, she gazed across the Arno with a sense of detachment. With a grunt, Adam stood up. Pulling her up and turning her around, he took her face in his hands and looked seriously at her, his eyes almost black.

'My God, Sofia that was incredible,' his eyes roamed her face for signs of her reaction. Stretching up to kiss him she said, 'for once I have to agree with you, Mr. Flynn.' Bending down to retrieve her clothes, a sense of liberation swept through her. If she could be here, in Florence, making love to Adam, then anything was possible! She stood up with a grin as wide as the Arno. 'Come on you. I think we should test out that bedroom for lovers', and taking him by the hand led him down the stairs.

LE PASSEGGIATE MANO A MANO

(Walks hand in hand)

Adam woke early on Saturday and left Sofia sleeping soundly, splayed out, and taking up an inordinate amount of room for such a tiny person. He padded up to the kitchen to get some juice but when he opened the fridge door thought, "sod it" and moved across to the counter to turn on the coffee machine. Looking through the pods in the bowl, he picked up one marked cappuccino, revelling in this freedom from restrictions. Sipping the frothy brew, he turned on his phone, starting guiltily when he saw missed calls from his dad. It was the middle of the night back in Texas he worked out, and resolved to call him later. His guilt did nothing to trouble his contentedness as he marvelled at the events of last night.

They had made love again, on that sumptuous bed, less frantic but no less intense. Talking into the early hours, she had drifted off in his arms and he'd lain there, fighting sleep, savouring the sensation. Hearing sounds of movement downstairs, he prepared an espresso and carefully carried it down for Sofia. She was pulling on a t-shirt when he walked in, but stopped, looking self-conscious.

'I made you this,' he said, placing it on the dresser.

'Thanks, I was just coming to get some…' she replied as she finished getting dressed. He watched her, wondering if she regretted last night, his heart sinking at the thought. He sat on the bed, unsure of how to proceed and feeling out of his depth.

'Sofia, are you OK? Are we OK?' he asked. She smiled at him and walked over, inserting herself between his knees and wrapping her arms around him. 'We are more than OK, Adam. She whispered, kissing the top of his head. It was just weird for a moment; this whole situation is so new.'

He held on to her, thrilled that this was going somewhere. 'It's new for both of us, but we can just take it one day at a time,' he said into her stomach, breathing in the heady scent of her. She pulled back to look at him, her face radiant. 'We can,' she said happily, 'and this day will comprise of me drinking that coffee over there, then us going on the tour I have organised. It's about time we saw some culture!'

☼

They strolled, hand in hand, through the bustling streets towards the iconic red dome to meet the guide. They spotted her straight away, a tall, elegantly dressed woman in her late thirties with a shining bob of auburn hair.

'Good morning, my name is Anastasia,' she said in accented English 'are you ready to "experience" Florence?'

Entering the Cathedral of Santa Maria del Fiore, Anastasia explained its chequered history. 'They placed the first stone of the facade on 8 September 1296 and it was the largest cathedral in Europe at the time of its completion in the 15th century.' They walked over the intricately tiled floors, talking in hushed voices. As they approached the 3 frescoes alongside the left nave, Sofia let out a gasp of wonder, her hand clamping to her mouth as she took in the incredible works of art.

Seeing that she was particularly drawn to one, the guide stood beside her. 'Dante Before the City of Florence by Domenico di

Michelino,' she said. 'It is especially interesting because it shows us, apart from scenes of the Divine Comedy, a view on Florence in 1465, which is something he could not have seen.' They gazed up in wonder at the elaborate paintings within the Dome itself, before Anastasia led them up the stairs of Giotto's bell tower to see the best views in the city.

'This is awesome,' Adam said, looking out across the panorama of the city.

'Nearly as good as the view I had last night.' Sofia replied with a wink. Images of their time on the roof flashed through his mind, and he felt a surge of lust. Laughing at his weakness for this girl, Adam tried to concentrate on what Anastasia was telling them. She was a wonderful guide, friendly, humorous, knowledgeable, and her obvious passion for the city shone through as she reeled off information about the streets as they walked through.

The next stop was Accademia Gallery, primarily for Michelangelo's sculpture of David, before they went to the Uffizi. 'OK,' said Anastasia once they entered the courtyard of the museum, 'we could lose hours exploring in here. Are there any works of art or artists that you simply must not miss?'

'Botticelli and Caravaggio' said Sofia instantly. 'I can't wait to see Birth of Venus!'

'I'm easy,' said Adam, amazed at Sofia's knowledge, 'I'm not really an art buff.'

They made their way from room to room, Adam taking vicarious pleasure from Sofia's excitement at each discovery. She was in heaven, bouncing from one to the other, like a pinball on speed. Sofia felt like the luckiest person on the planet; this day couldn't get any better. When they'd seen their fill, Anastasia took them to the café on the first floor, a welcome respite after the walking they had done. With a beautiful outdoor terrace and an incredible view over the Piazza della Signoria and the Palazzo Vecchio, it was the perfect end to their tour.

'So, how did you find it?' asked Anastasia after placing their order for drinks. 'I understand from your emails, Sofia, that you are looking for tours to recommend to your clients?'

Sofia nodded enthusiastically. 'I loved it; you have such amazing knowledge. I think our members would love a curated tour like this. What do you think?' she asked, looking at Adam.

'Absolutely,' he agreed. 'It's just the kind of thing we are looking for,' he smiled across at her.

Anastasia stood, handing them both her business card 'Well I have to be off, I have another tour this afternoon, but it was lovely to meet you both.' Adam gave her a discreetly folded note as he shook her hand, 'we'll be in touch' he said.

'Shall we stay here and have lunch?' Sofia asked once the woman had left, she'd been avidly watching plates of food arriving at neighbouring tables. Smiling and nudging her foot with his under the table he said, 'I was wondering how long it would be until you mentioned food.'

They spent a wonderful couple of hours admiring the view and people watching, sipping on Aperol Spritzers. Eventually, Adam said, 'Come on, we'd better go. If we're here any longer, we'll have to order dinner as well!'

Sofia looked up, a frown wrinkling her brow. 'It's Saturday, isn't it? I completely forgot I'm having dinner with Uncle Joey tonight.' Her face fell. 'sorry Adam, I was looking forward to us spending the entire day together.' She touched his hand lying on the table, her face a picture of concern.

'I'm a big boy,' he said, smiling at her. 'I can fend for myself for one evening. There's some work to catch up on and I wanted to call my dad, so it's fine,' he reassured her.

☼

As she got ready to go out that evening, she was excited. It had been so many years since she'd seen her uncle, and she was looking forward to dinner with anticipation. Adam wolf-whistled when she walked into the lounge. 'Are you sure it's your uncle you're meeting?' he asked, openly appraising the body-fitting black dress that she was wearing. Exulting under his wanton gaze, she walked over and bent down to kiss him. He was stretched out on one of the sofas, laptop resting on his stomach; glasses perched on the end of his nose.

'I will see you later, mister,' she said 'I'm going to wait downstairs; Uncle Joey is picking me up soon.' He watched her walk away, down the hall, giving him a last brief wave before she closed the door. He couldn't believe the fortune that had brought her into his life; he'd felt more alive these last days than at any point before and he was determined not to let go of that feeling.

His phone rang, and he stretched a lazy arm out to pick it up off the coffee table, holding his laptop in place with the other.

'There you are!' said Jack, with no preamble.

'Hi, Pop,' said Adam, sitting up and pushing his glasses back into place. 'Sorry I missed your calls yesterday, I was busy.'

'I was worried, Son; it's not like you to turn your phone off.'

'I know, I know. I really am sorry for causing you concern but everything is fine.'

'Well, I was calling you to tell you about that Joey you were asking about. He's a right shady character, fingers in lots of pies.'

'What sort of pies?' Adam asked, sitting up straighter and awkwardly moving his laptop to the table with one hand.

'In Galveston, he had an antiques store but my sources say it was a cover for a money laundering business. They are pretty sure he was fencing stolen artwork as well.'

'Did the cops get close to catching him?' Adam asked.

'Well, they did. An undercover agent was right in with him, setting up a deal. But that's the thing, Son, they disappeared.'

'Who, Joey?'

'No, the agent. Vanished without a trace, the same day Joey Russo flew off to Italy, never to return.'

Adam stared into the middle distance, mind racing. Did Sofia know how dangerous her uncle was? Or was she oblivious to his nefarious activities? He couldn't imagine her complicity in such things.

☼

'Ciao, Bella,' said Uncle Joey, leaning over from the driver's seat to give her a bristly kiss. 'Look at you, all grown up, you're a woman now!' he exclaimed.

Sofia laughed. 'Oh, Zio. It's so good to see you,' she said happily, clicking her seatbelt into place. 'So, where are we going for dinner?' she asked as he pulled out into the traffic.

'A little place I know,' he said dismissively. 'Tell me everything. How are things in Galveston, the family, your new job?'

As Uncle Joey easily manoeuvred the car through the narrow streets, alive with Saturday night celebrants, Sofia brought him up to date on the goings-on. Her excitement at her new job, the restaurant's new lunchtime schedule, and the battle of wits that had erupted between Aldo and her father. Joey laughed. 'Aldo was always more like your father than the rest of you,' he said as he pulled the car to a stop in a side street. He switched off the engine and looked at her 'you have always been more like my dear sister; Valentina always had a good head on her shoulders.'

She took his arm as they walked around the corner to the restaurant. 'Here we are,' he said, pausing outside a dark wood entrance. Sofia looked up; over the door in gold letters was the name Cibrèo Ristorante.

'Oh! I've heard of this place. I'm sure I read about it online. It's supposed to be one of the best places to eat in Florence,' she said, looking at her uncle with joy.

'It certainly is, Piccolo, that's why we are here!'

Laughing, she made her way inside, eager to see the interior and taste the food. The dark wood of the entrance continued inside. The well-polished floor and ornate bar and display cabinets in the same antique wood, offset beautifully by the glowing ochre walls. Each table was magnificently set, a posy of bright yellow chrysanthemums joyfully taking centre place. They were greeted by a young waiter with a serious expression.

'Signor Russo.' He said, bowing his head slightly.

'Ciao Mario, I hope all is well with you? I have a table booked for my niece and I.'

Mario nodded and showed them to their table, and once they were settled took their drinks order. Joey reeled off a name of a bottle of wine with a much-practised air and requested Champagne Cocktails to kick off the evening. Mario returned with two chilled flute glasses, a sugar cube nestling in the base and fizzing away in each.

The sparkling wine had a sweet and sour taste, Sofia noted as she took her first sip, looking around the restaurant and taking everything in.

'It's a wonderful place, Zio,' she said to her uncle, who had already finished his champagne and was pouring glasses of wine. He looked up at her and smiled. 'I'm glad you like it. It's become one of my favourite places to dine since I returned to Italy.'

Looking thoughtful, Sofia put her glass back on the table, wondering how to ask the question that had been in the back of her mind for years.

'Tell me something,' she began, looking at him hopefully 'why did you leave? Why did you go so suddenly? One day you were there and the next, poof,' she said with a sad smile. Her parents had mumbled something unsatisfactory about his wanting to retire; their reticence to expand on the subject told her there was more to this story.

'It's complicated, Sofia.' He replied enigmatically, sipping his wine.

'Try me.' She insisted. 'Whatever went on, I am old enough to deal with it now.'

He gazed into her eyes for a moment before looking away with a small shake of his head. 'All you need to know was that I did it for love,' he stated, gazing off into a memory. He looked back, 'and that is all I am prepared to tell you about this matter, so drop it,' he said sharply. Looking contrite, Sofia nodded meekly. Her uncle had never raised his voice to her before; she felt tears welling up and tried to stifle them.

Unabashed, Uncle Joey looked around and waved over a smartly dressed woman who came and pulled up a seat at their table.

'Ciao, Christina, stai bene?' he asked, before introducing her to Sofia. Christina explained to Sofia that as the menu at Cibrèo changed daily, depending on the season and what was available, they didn't have menus. She went on in great detail to explain the mouth-watering dishes that were available that evening, distracting Sofia almost completely from the conversation she'd just had with her uncle. But a small part of her mind was resolved to find out more about that story.

After much debate, they decided to have the yellow bell pepper soup, a classic beef ragout with ricotta and potato dumplings followed by bitter orange cheesecake for Sofia and a raspberry tart for Joey. Confirming they had no allergies that the chef should be aware of, Christina left to take their order to the kitchen, leaving an awkward silence in their wake.

Eventually, Sofia asked, 'So, tell me about your life here. Do you still deal in antiques?'

A broad smile erupted over his craggy face. 'Of course, Bambino, you know they are of the greatest importance to me, next to food and music,' he laughed. 'I no longer have a shop. But I have a storeroom and do the market circuit throughout Tuscany. If you have time you should come, they are wonderful.' He sat back to allow Mario to serve their first course, thanking him before continuing. 'I have a little place just outside of Siena and travel all over the region, it is a wonderful life.'

As she listened to him, she could see the sparkle in his eyes, the joy of what he was living self-evident, and she realised that whatever had caused him to come back to Italy, it had been a good move.The rest of the meal passed in good company, both of them savouring each plate as it arrived. The surprisingly large portions left Sofia feeling bloated, but she didn't leave a crumb. She imagined Adam laughing at her appetite and smiled.

'What's making you so happy?' her quick-witted uncle asked, 'surely not just an old man's company and a good meal?' Debating for a second, but her excitement overcoming any fears, she looked at him with shining eyes. 'I have met someone, Zio, a man,' she blurted before she changed her mind.

'Well, that's good to hear,' he said sagely 'where is he from?'

Realising in an instant he was referring to the man's Italian family heritage, she shook her head 'he's not Italian. He's from Houston, an Irish family. His dad was a cop.'

Uncle Joey paused mid-sip, his eyes clouding over. 'Be careful, Piccolo,' he said seriously, 'it can be difficult mixing cultures like this, especially with people who think they have the law on their side,' he said darkly.

Feeling deflated, Sofia didn't want to talk about Adam anymore. She didn't want anything tainting her joyful bubble, so she asked him about his upcoming market, Fortezza Antiquaria, which was here in Florence.

'It was good timing,' he said happily 'I get to take part in my favourite market and see my favourite niece at the same time. This reminds me, I have a gift for you in the car.' He lifted his glass 'to family' he said. Dutifully raising her glass and muttering a response, Sofia was wondering if she could convince Adam to go to the market tomorrow. If Uncle Joey met him, she was sure he would feel better about the relationship. And it would be good practise for Adam before he met her brothers, something she knew they were going to have to face if they carried on seeing each other.

It was late when they arrived outside the apartment. Uncle Joey got out of the car with her, opened the boot, and pointed inside. A dark, antique-looking violin case was there in the glow of the lights. 'Go on, open it,' he said, eyes sparkling. Tentatively, she reached in and snapped open the locks, holding it closed. She took a breath as she lifted the lid, her senses telling her that something wonderful was inside.

Her senses were right. Sitting snuggly in the case was a beautiful instrument, its polished lustre a yellow-brown that suggested maple, and the scroll was finely carved. Gingerly, she lifted it out, turning it to take in its form.

'It's wonderful,' she breathed, unable to take her eyes off it.

'It's a "Gabrielli", made in the 18th century,' he said proudly.

'Oh, Zio, it must have cost a fortune,' she said, looking at him in wonder. 'I can't accept something like this!'

'I won't hear anything of the sort,' he said genially, 'take it, play it and enjoy it. That is why they are made. Not to be stuck in a showcase somewhere, never to be heard – that's an actual crime if you ask me.' He finished with a mirthless laugh.

Placing it reverently back in its case, she turned and enveloped him in a hug. 'I will try to do it justice, Zio,' she said, on the brink of tears at this generous gesture.

Tiptoeing into the apartment, she saw Adam was already asleep in the master bedroom. She stood smiling at his sleeping form for a moment before taking the violin to what had originally been her room and placing it on the bed. Quickly washing her face and brushing her teeth, she pulled on an oversized t-shirt and went back to Adam. Snuggling in next to him and sliding her arms around him, her mind wandered over the conversation with her uncle, trying to make sense of it as she drifted off to sleep.

☼

The next morning, Adam woke with a start, dragged from a dream of shady characters and murky goings-on. There was no sign of Sofia, so he walked to the other bedroom to see if she was in there getting dressed. Opening the door, he registered a violin case on the bed just as he heard the front door being opened. 'Adam, are you up?' Sofia called out 'I went to get some croissants for breakfast.'

Following the sound of her voice, they met in the lounge and she reached up to kiss him, waving the bakery bag at him, the scent of freshly baked pastries reaching his nose. They sat at the polished kitchen counter, devouring their breakfast as Sofia regaled him with the meal she had eaten last night. The conversation with his father still reverberating, Adam could only grunt in response, finding it hard to be enthusiastic about anything that concerned her family.

He was looking through his emails when he paused, rereading whatever had caught his attention. 'Sofia, what pictures have you put on your Instagram?' he asked, his voice low. Surprised at his tone, she grabbed her phone and opened it, holding it up for him to see.

'Just a few shots of our tour, lots of food, of course, and a few of the apartment. See?'

He looked as she scrolled down, his face twisting with an emotion she couldn't fathom. 'Well, Peter has emailed me asking about the apartment on your feed, asking why I haven't given him the details as it looks perfect.'

He was writhing with anger, his carefully curated selection of apartments seemingly being dismissed in an instant. All that hard work wasted, his opinion obviously counting for nothing!

'Well, I could ask Zio Joey if he would be interested in renting if you like?' she asked hesitantly, feeling the waves of anger washing off of him.

'You knew I didn't want to suggest this one. You have done this deliberately, haven't you!' he spat, pushing back his stool and towering over her.

'Don't be ridiculous, Adam,' she shot back, refusing to be cowed. 'I was just showing my friends and family my adventures.'

'Oh yes, your precious family,' he snarled, and stalked downstairs to his room.

She sat, stunned, unsure what to do. Shock at his reaction soon gave way to anger. How dare he speak to her like that? Making a decision, she picked up her bag and stormed out of the apartment, shoving the front door shut with a resounding slam that echoed down the stairs.

A BUON INTENDITOR, POCHE PAROLE

(A word to the wise

In his room, Adam knew he had completely overreacted. His anger had surprised him. It left him shaking, but the fact that he had upset Sofia affected him even more. He took a long shower, trying to get a grip on his emotions and make sense of the situation. His natural response to the information his father had told him the previous evening was to steer clear of Sofia and anything to do with her family, but he couldn't imagine his life without her now. How he had fallen so hard, so quickly, he didn't know. A week ago, he wouldn't have thought it possible.

As he towelled himself dry, he wondered what he could do to resolve the situation and realised that he couldn't achieve anything without talking to her. He sent her a message, apologising for his reaction and asking her to come back to the apartment so they could talk. That done, he opened his laptop to try to do some work. All he could do now was wait.

Sofia didn't even open the message from Adam. She was far too angry right now to listen to anything he had to say. As she wandered around the market at Piazza Indipendenza, looking for her uncle, she soon became lost in the stalls and the amazing antiques on offer. Winding her way through the market, discovering her way through treasures ranging from furniture to knick-knacks, books and collectables, went some way towards distracting her, but the image of him snarling at her insisted on popping into her head, making her angry all over again.

She found Uncle Joey chatting amiably with some customers, and his face lit up when he saw her.

'*Buongiorno*, Piccolo,' he said, coming over to hug her. 'How are you today?'

'*Buongiorno, Zio*, I've been better,' she replied sourly.

Taking in her angry countenance in surprise - this was so unlike his happy, go-lucky niece - he made a quick decision.

'Give me a moment to finish with these customers,' he said, giving her shoulders a squeeze 'then we'll get a coffee and you can tell me all about it.'

Smiling gratefully, she nodded and stood, idly picking up pieces from his stand and looking at them while he finished making the sale. Once the customers were dealt with, he called over to the woman at the next stall, asking her to watch his stand whilst he was away, and took Sofia's hand and lead her to the busy coffee shop on the other side of the market.

Sitting in the bright sunlight, she explained to him the conversation with Adam, his ridiculous accusation that she was somehow trying to outdo him, and her disbelief of his angry backlash.

Joey chuckled. 'Relationships with someone you work with are always tricky.' He said, sipping his coffee. 'You have injured his pride, Piccolo; you have inadvertently come up with the perfect apartment, which by the sounds of it was an important victory for him.'

Sofia sat back in her seat, pulling her sunglasses off and placing them on the table as she digested his words. 'Oh, you are probably right,' she said, regarding him, 'but what can I do, it was an accident. I was focused on finding tours for the program, not apartments. He should just be thankful we have somewhere to stay!'

'Well, let us say that I am not interested in renting the place, which is a shame, as it could have been lucrative, but for now, tell your boss the apartment is not on the table. That puts this man back in control of the situation.'

'That hardly seems fair to you,' she said, her face screwed up in consternation. He shrugged and finished his coffee.

'Figurati,' he said simply, 'it is what it is. Now I have to get back to work. I tell you what, tomorrow I have been invited to go on a wine tasting tour. Why don't you come with me? You can give him some space to continue with his quest and do your job at the same time.'

Relief that she had a plan that would make Adam happy washed over her and she nodded eagerly. 'I'm still mad at him, but yes, that sounds like a lovely idea.'

They both stood and slowly made their way back to his stall, Joey stopping to chat to people he knew along the way. When they reached it, Sofia kissed him on his cheek. 'Thank you, Zio. You are a very wise man,' she said with a smile. He laughed. 'I'm not so sure, but I'm glad I could help. Now I will see you early tomorrow, I will pick you up and we can have a wonderful day together!'

Determined not to go rushing back to Adam - he could sit and stew for a while as far as she was concerned - Sofia meandered through the streets, soaking in the atmosphere. It was a beautiful day, and the city was thronging with tourists and locals alike. She stopped at a small trattoria and had a bite to eat, revelling in her worldliness. A woman dining alone in Florence, who would have thought Sofia Marino would ever do such a thing!

☼

It was late afternoon by the time she got back, slowly opening the door, unsure of her welcome. She needn't have worried. Adam bounded over like a dog left too long in his enthusiasm, engulfing her in a hug.

'I am so sorry, Sofia,' he murmured into her hair. 'I was a complete jackass.'

She laughed, relief flooding through her. 'You were, and it's something we will definitely talk about, but for now, come with me.' She led him towards the bedroom, both of them speeding up as they reached the doorway, before tumbling onto the bed in a tangle of limbs.

They decided to eat at Stefano's restaurant again, neither of them wanting to stray too far that evening. The argument still sat between them, both of them not wanting to spoil the atmosphere after the wonderful make up sex. They chatted easily, while enjoying their Pollo alla Fiorentina, a heavenly concoction of chicken and spinach in a creamy garlic sauce, and drinking a very palatable Chianti. It was only when Stefano had cleared away the remains of the meal that Sofia broached the subject.

'So, Adam,' Sofia began as she passed her plate to Stefano, 'just so you know, I have emailed Peter and told him that the apartment upstairs is not an option for City Breaks.'

Adam's head snapped up, and he stared at her. He felt his anger swirling dangerously close to the surface. 'Why did you do that?'

'I thought that's what you wanted?' she replied, not liking the look on his face.

'What I wanted was for you to leave things well alone and stop sticking your nose into what is essentially my business,' he snapped, slapping his napkin down on the table and pushing his chair back. His face flushed, his eyes glittered. 'What you need to remember is that you are the assistant, Sofia.'

'What you need to remember is I was just trying to help, and you are being a jackass again!' she shouted, causing the other diners to gawk at them. Feeling his control slipping, Adam stood and made for the door. He would not lose his cool anymore, he had to escape. He ran up the stairs and into the apartment, making straight for the bedroom that he'd first slept in, shutting the door and leaning against it, panting.

What was it about Sofia? She rattled him silly and brought out feelings that he just couldn't control. He went and sat on the bed, feeling drained. Looking around the room, he decided he would spend the night in here rather than risk further confrontations... Or sex. He had to straighten his head out. Things were spinning out of control and he was going to screw everything up if he didn't take back a hold of this trip and his life.

Sofia sat, staring at the restaurant door that closed behind Adam, unable to get her head around this sudden switch in their relationship. Stefano rushed over 'is everything alright?' he asked quietly.

'Yes, and no,' she sniffed, determined not to cry, 'we just had a disagreement is all.'

He rubbed her back sympathetically. 'Let me get you a brandy. Sit here for a bit, give him time to cool down.'

'A brandy would be great, but as far as I'm concerned, he can go to hell. I rushed into this relationship. I should have known better than to get involved with a man I hardly know, no matter how attractive he is.'

She sipped her drink, gazing out at the street, watching lovers stroll by hand in hand. She would have to talk to him, she thought sadly; tell him things were over between them. There was no point going on, she couldn't be with someone who reacted that way every time he felt he wasn't in control. She still didn't understand why he was behaving so weirdly, it just didn't make sense. She thought of the amazing moments they'd shared, the fun they had, how well they worked together. It was a shame; she had thought he was the one. She paid the bill with a sad smile and went up to find him. The apartment was silent, Adam nowhere to be seen, and the door to his bedroom resolutely closed.

"God, he's such a child," she thought to herself as she walked to her room. Seeing the violin on the bed, she brightened. 'At least I have a day with Uncle Joey tomorrow,' she said to the instrument as she put it away in the wardrobe. Looking in the bathroom mirror as she brushed her teeth, she was relieved she had something to do the next day. Let Adam do his "business" and she would do hers.

☼

She slipped out the door quietly early the next morning to go and meet her uncle. She left Adam a note to say she was spending the day with him, trying out a tour, before eagerly escaping. The street was a little chilly, the sun barely up, and she pulled her cardigan around herself more firmly to try and generate some warmth. Her uncle's car soon slid into view and she got into its welcome warmth with a smile.

The roads were fairly quiet at this time of the morning, and Joey easily traversed the city. Sofia sat mostly in silence, lost in thought, watching the streets pass by. Twenty minutes later she became aware they were passing signs for the airport and sure enough, when they reached the entrance, he indicated and pulled onto the road that led to the main terminal.

'Where exactly are we going, Zio?' she asked, turning her head to look at him. He glanced at her, his face bright with excitement 'I said we were going on a tour, I didn't say how we were getting there!' he said gleefully. Laughing at his childish glee, she looked ahead, wondering what on earth he could be playing at. When he finally pulled to a stop, it was next to a sign declaring 'Eliporto' and she could see a smart, silver and black helicopter out on the tarmac.

'*Oddio!*' she exclaimed softly, her face now mirroring his with excitement. 'Really?'

'Yes, really, little one,' he chuckled. 'If you are going to see Tuscany, then you should see it like a bird, from the sky!'

Shaking her head in disbelief, she followed him over to where the smartly dressed captain, a rugged-looking man in his late fifties, was standing by to greet them and help them in. Anticipation building, she strapped herself in and dutifully listened to the brief safety advice from the captain. As the rotors started, the noise becoming deafening, Joey waved at the headphones on the seat next to her and she slid them over her ears. Unlike on the plane, she had no trepidation, even when the helicopter lurched into the air. Gazing out of the window in rapture as it lifted higher, before crossing back over Florence, all thoughts of Adam disappeared.

The Tuscan countryside unrolled beneath them, jaw-droppingly beautiful, with never-ending greens punctuated with ochre hued hamlets. The captain kept up a running commentary as they flew over the Chianti Classico hills, pointing out the various castles and towns of note. All too soon, he was telling them they were about to land, hovering for a few moments before gently bringing them down on the helipad at Tenuta Torciano Winery. Stepping out of the helicopter, Sofia took a deep breath. The countryside was magnificent and the air rejuvenating.

'What did you think of the ride, Sofia?' Uncle Joey asked, coming to join her as they both watched the approach of a white golf buggy.

She slapped his shoulder playfully. 'You know full well it was amazing,' she replied. 'I cannot imagine a better way to see this amazing scenery.'

The buggy juddered to a halt in front of them, and a young man with a toothpaste advert smile jumped out to greet them, hand out, ready to shake.

'Hi, my name is Gabriele,' he said happily, clasping Joey first, then Sofia. 'I will show you around a little before we have a tasting and we will have lunch as well. *Dai!*' His enthusiasm was infectious, and they eagerly jumped into the cart, Gabriele shouting over his shoulder at them as they bounced through the tracks of the vineyard, explaining the incredible heritage of the place, owned by the same family for over three hundred years.

It fascinated Sofia; she had known nothing about the science behind winemaking, and it astounded her in its complexity. As they made their way through the cellars, she tried to make a note of the information, but it was all a little much. Gabriele promised to send her some information after the tour so she could provide details to the guests coming to stay in Florence. Truffle hunting in the woods with a pair of enthusiastic terrier-type dogs made her laugh out loud, pure joy erupting at a successful find. Joey looked on; glad that this day had proved to be the distraction she needed from Adam.

☼

Adam, however, had no such distractions. Dragged from a deep sleep by his alarm, he'd padded down the hall to Sofia's room and knocked. Pushing the door open gently so as not to disturb her when there was no reply, it surprised him to find an empty room, an unmade bed and no sign of her anywhere. He found the note she had left on the coffee machine. Trying to read between the lines of the brief message, he didn't know whether to feel furious with her for abandoning their plan for second viewings today or relieved that he didn't have to face her.

As he watched the burst of coffee stream into his cup, he tried to focus his mind on the job ahead. He was meeting Andrea to look at two of the apartments again and start to go through contractual details to see which one would be the best fit. Jack had messaged overnight, giving more information about Joey Russo. Apparently, he had a house in Siena, but so far the local *Polizia* had no evidence of any illegal activities. Pushing thoughts of

Sofia's family firmly aside, Adam got dressed and went to meet the agent.

Despite Andrea's obvious disappointment at Sofia's absence, he soon rallied as he and Adam got into the nitty-gritty of what each property offered and what he knew the owners to be flexible on or not. Once he had thoroughly inspected both places, Adam suggested they go for lunch to discuss things further. Glancing at his phone for the hundredth time, he saw there was still no news from Sofia. He missed her. He couldn't untangle the mess of feelings that emerged when he thought about her, but he knew things weren't the same without her.

Andrea took him to his favourite place; Angel Roofbar spread over three floors of a hotel in the centre and had a fantastic, panoramic view. The shady terrace looked out over the skyline and even Adam, who was a little indifferent to the beauty of the place now, was jolted out of his apathy as they took their seats. The food was excellent, a perfect mix between Italian traditions and fusion cuisine expertly prepared and plated, but Adam had little appetite and just picked at his meal. Andrea, who'd had to do most of the talking today, took a moment out to look at his phone.

'Mio Dio!' he muttered, and Adam noticed raised voices around him, a Chinese whisper of some news sweeping across the terrace. 'What's going on?' he asked, unable to make sense of what little he could make out.

'There has been a robbery!' he looked up from his phone looking pale. 'They have hit UniCredit, two gunmen, look,' he held up his phone showing a news page, headline screaming "Il ritorno di Cosa Nostra." Underneath was a blurry CCTV camera image of a masked man, firing a Tommy gun in the air.

'Tell me what it says,' he urged Andrea, who had taken back his phone and was scrolling through the page. 'It says they hurt no one,' he uttered, eyes still glued to the screen, involuntarily crossing himself. 'Two men, the leader did all the talking, shot out the cameras, and frightened the life outta everyone. The other one didn't say a word, just stuffed all the money in the bags before they made a break for it.'

Adam slumped back in his seat, his mind racing. This sounded awfully familiar. His phone rang, and he knew exactly who it would be. 'Hey, Pop,' he answered, wondering what time it was in Houston.

'Have you heard the news?' Jack blurted.

'Yes, just hearing it now. How come you know already?'

'One of my buddies at the station called to tell me, he knew I'd be interested. It's exactly the same MO as the one that happened here,' Jack went on excitedly, 'same guns, same silent partner and same vanishing act. What does Sofia Marino have to say about it?'

Adam had a flash of the violin case he had seen on her bed yesterday. 'She's not here… Er, she's spending the day with her uncle.'

There was silence on the line as the implications sunk in. 'That's it!' Jack shouted eventually 'the second gunman wasn't a man, it was a woman. That's why they didn't speak, so as not to give it away!'

Adam sat in stunned silence, trying to think through everything he thought he knew about Sofia. She couldn't be involved, could she?

'I always knew I was missing an important fact,' Jack was crowing, 'but now I have it. I gotta go, son, check through my information again and see if I can piece together who the woman was.'

The line went dead and Adam slowly put his phone on the table, wondering if it was at all possible he had started a relationship with someone in the Mafia.

NON È TUTTO ORO QUELLO CHE LUCCICA

(All that glitters is not gold)

Sofia, oblivious to the news that was rocking the Italian media, was having a fantastic time. The lunch served at the winery was exquisite, plate after plate of sumptuous foods flavoured with truffles and paired with the best wines the valley offered. She was in seventh heaven and could have stayed there for a week.

'Thank you so much, Zio,' she said to her uncle as they strolled through the grounds after lunch. 'This is a remarkable place. I'm sure our members would love it, especially the transport' she giggled, still unable to believe she had flown in a helicopter.

'I am glad I have made you happy,' he smiled down at her and ruffled her hair affectionately. She ducked away from the childhood gesture, but there was a grin on her face. She thought about Adam. it was a shame he had missed this. His taste buds could have done with the workout. Truffles, garlic, balsamic vinegars and glorious cheeses. It would have done him the world of good. A frown clouded her face, flitting across as she thought of the conversation she was going to have with him when she got back.

Her phone chimed to signal an incoming message, and she

eagerly pulled it out of her pocket, aware of the butterflies breaking out in her stomach at the thought it might be Adam. Her face drained of all colour as she read it.

'What is it, Piccolo?' asked Joey, seeing the torment on her face.

'Mamma,' she whispered, passing him the phone and sinking to her knees. She heard his sharp intake of breath, his shouting instructions to someone, and was aware of his gentle hands lifting her to her feet and leading her to the helicopter.

'Sofia,' he said as they boarded, 'Sofia,' he said again sharply when she didn't respond. She looked at him with wounded eyes. 'Do you have your passport with you?' he demanded urgently. She nodded mutely, aware of him shouting again into his *telefano* now, making travel arrangements.

☼

Adam was waiting for her at the apartment, pacing the length of the grand salon, running various conversations through his mind.

"So, Sofia, rob any good banks today?" he chuckled maniacally. He was definitely losing his grip. When evening came and she still hadn't returned or responded to his calls, he began to worry. A steady drip of doubt trickled through his mind. What if something had happened to her? Her phone had been switched off for hours, which wasn't normal. Her note had said she would be back late afternoon, and it was well into evening now. He opened the door to her room, taking in her possessions still in place, and trying to ignore the fact that he couldn't see the violin case.

He called his dad; he didn't know what else to do – he certainly wasn't going to the police… Not yet, anyway.

'Hi Pop, it's me,' he said in strained tones 'did you say you had an address for Joey Russo?'

'Yes, son, I've got it right here. Hold on, there was a ping as the message came through. I've sent it to you. Why do you want it?'

'I'm just worried about Sofia, she hasn't come back.'

'You want to go to his place? Accuse him of what?' Jack retorted. 'Don't be stupid, Adam, the last person who tried to get close to him disappeared without a trace. I forbid you to go down there.'

'I'm just thinking ahead, Pops. If she's not back by morning, then at least I can give the local police some information,' Adam said, fingers firmly crossed. Pacified, Jack said, 'I'll email you what else I have on him, just in case it's useful.'

Adam intended to wait until morning, but planned to drive there himself. He pulled out his laptop and located the nearest car hire company. A quick phone call later and he had arranged for it to be dropped off in an hour. He glanced through the email his father had sent, startled to notice the investigating officer who had disappeared was a woman, Anna Rathbourne. Her picture was included, a woman in her late fifties with chic blonde hair, a mischievous sparkle in her blue eyes despite the serious pose of the photo.

He tried Sofia's phone again, leaving another voice message. Looking around, he didn't know what else he could do. He resumed pacing, unable to think of eating or doing anything until he knew what had happened to Sofia. The thought of her being in trouble, no matter what she was mixed up in, was driving him crazy. The buzzer sounded, and he jumped out of his skin. Checking the time, he saw an hour had passed, and he ran down quickly to take delivery of the car. When he came back up, keys in hand, he stood for a moment, running his hand through his hair, staring at the wall.

'Sod this' he said to the room and scooped up his phone, put the address into Maps and saw Siena was an hour away. He grabbed a bottle of water and his wallet and flew down the stairs. There was no way he could sit passively by, waiting for something to happen. He knew Sofia needed him, he could just feel it.

The hour-long drive took nearer to two, wrong turns and roadworks all doing their best to detain him. When he finally pulled into the driveway, he whistled. The impressive building became visible in the distance; discreet uplights making it glow between the Cyprus trees that lined the winding drive that seemed to stretch for miles.

He pulled the cord on the old-fashioned bell to the right of the impressive front door, hewn from huge chunks of aged oak; it was a herald of what lay behind it. A small woman opened the door, her dark, lined face bellying her age and time spent in the sun.

'*Si, Signore?*' she asked, looking him up and down.

'*Buonasera, signora,*' he began uncertainly, the stress-fuelled urgency of getting here receding in the house's grandeur, 'I am looking for *Signore* Russo?'

'*Un minuto,*' she replied and firmly closed the door in his face.

Adam stepped back, looking up at the house. It looked to be an old farmhouse, or maybe an olive press. The restoration was well done and screamed of money. The door was opened again, by a different woman this time. She was tall and slim, but unlike the previous woman, her face was unmarked by the passage of time, just a hint of crow's feet around her blue eyes.

'I believe you are looking for my husband?' she asked, surprising him with her American accent, 'can I ask what this is about?'

Returning her direct gaze, he decided there was no point in inscrutability. 'Yes, of course. I am looking for Sofia Marino, his niece. She went out with him today and hasn't returned and I can't reach her by phone.'

Tilting her head to one side, she considered him for a moment, tucking a strand of dark hair behind her ear, before saying, 'in that case I can tell you he is on his way to Houston, his sister has been rushed to hospital.'

'Oh God, poor Sofia,' he said, heart sinking at what she must be going through, all thoughts of bank robberies flying out the window.

'Can I ask who you are?' the woman asked, still looking at him with unblinking, intelligent eyes.

'My name is Adam, I work with Sofia,' he answered, not wanting to give any more weight to their relationship.

'Ah yes, you were staying at Joey's apartment with her. Come in for a moment, you can actually help me with something.' She turned without waiting for a response and led him through to a beautiful living space, high beams and arched brickwork confirming his earlier thoughts of the building's heritage. She pointed at the sofas placed in an L shape to frame the cosy area by the fireplace. 'Take a seat, I will ask Maria to bring us something to drink; you look like you need it.'

He did as he was told, slowly lowering himself onto the seat, feeling completely drained. The emotional roller coaster of the last few days was finally taking its toll, and he leaned back and closed his eyes.

He opened them again when he heard the tap-tap of her heels returning, and she smiled at him. 'Maria will be here shortly,' she said, tucking her skirt under her as she took her seat on the other sofa.'

'Thank you,' he said, feeling displaced in this grand place with this cool, elegant woman.

'Joey asked me to go to the apartment to pack up Sofia's things,' she said, giving a slight nod to the maid as she came in with a tray containing a bottle of Vecchia Romagna brandy and two crystal glasses. 'He wants me to forward their suitcases with the service he uses, but there is something he wants you to take personally.'

Confused, Adam sat forward, repositioning his glasses before taking a slug of the brandy that Maria had poured. 'What's that, her laptop?' he asked. It was the only thing of any value he could come up with.

The woman laughed, a mischievous sparkle appearing in her

eyes. 'Hardly,' she scoffed, taking her first sip. 'He gave her a new violin, it's a Giovanni Battista Gabrielli which is worth a small fortune.' She placed her glass back on the coffee table and returned the look he was giving her.

'What's your name?' he asked abruptly, his mind now racing.

'You can call me Annabella' she said, looking away discomforted.

'Anna,' he said and her head snapped back, eyes wide 'you're Anna Rathbourne aren't you?'

Her already pale skin whitened further, her jaw clenched as she glared at him 'how could you possibly know that?' she demanded.

'It's a long story, but basically, my dad's a cop,' Adam replied, shaking his head trying to make sense of it all. 'What are you doing here? Everyone thought you had been killed, buried somewhere.'

'That was the plan, ya'll were supposed to forget about me,' she said, standing to top up their glasses. 'I guess I always knew I'd be found one day,' she said sadly as she sat back down.

'Adam, before you go rushing off to tell anyone, can I explain?'

He chuckled, taking another drink and realising the brandy was going straight to his head. He hadn't eaten much all day. 'You may as well,' he said 'I've heard enough insane stories for one day, another won't make much difference!'

'I was working undercover, as you probably know. Trying to get close enough to Joey to get some proof that he was money laundering. But the crazy thing is, the closer I got, the less evidence I could find... And the closer I got, the more we fell in love.' She looked at him, trying to see if he understood.

'That doesn't explain the vanishing act. Why didn't you just report your findings and carry on with your lives?'

'I was married,' she said blandly, 'not only that, I was married to the chief of police and he is not a nice man. Let's just say if I hadn't run away, I would have had to kill him, most likely in self-defence. He wasn't shy of slapping me around when he wasn't happy, and trust me, that man is never happy.'

'So you came up with the plan to escape?'

'Believe me, Adam, it was the only way. For my sanity and for our love, meeting Joey showed me what love was. I don't think I knew before then,'

Lost in thought, Adam finished his brandy then he said, 'why did he give Sofia a violin?'

'She plays like an angel apparently,' Anna replied, 'you don't know her very well do you?'

'I thought I did,' Adam murmured, wishing she was here now, that he could talk to her and straighten everything out.

'When do you fly back?' Anna asked, breaking into his reverie.

'With everything that has happened I am going to get the first flight can,' he said decisively, pulling his phone out of his pocket 'I need to be there for Sofia.'

'In that case, you should stay here tonight,' Anna said with a warm smile, pouring him more brandy, 'we can both go to the apartment tomorrow and get things organised.'

☼

As the plane circled to await its landing slot, Sofia shook her uncle awake. 'We're nearly there,' she said as he came around. 'How you managed to sleep I don't know,' she said.

'It comes with age, Sofia. There's a time for action and a time to sleep.'

'I am too worried about Mamma,' she replied, twisting her rings and looking pensively out of the window.

'And you think I'm not?' he bristled, looking angry.

'I didn't mean that,' she said, turning back to him and rubbing his shoulder 'I know how much you love her.'

Settling back down in his seat, he glanced at his watch. 'We'll be there any minute and Aldo will meet us. We will soon know the news.'

When she spotted her brother, Sofia raced through the crowd and threw herself into his arms, weeping, finally letting it all out.

'It's OK, Sofia, she's Ok,' he rubbed her back reassuringly. 'She had us worried for a bit, but she's a fighter. It was just a small heart attack, apparently.' Taking strength from his solid form and his words, she pulled back, wiping her face with her sleeve. Joey stepped in and embraced his nephew for a long minute. '*Bentornato, Zio*. It's good to have you back,' said Aldo, a little glassy-eyed. 'I wish it was under happier circumstances but we are all glad you are here.'

'I am thrilled to see you again, Aldo, but can we hurry? I want to see my sister!'

Valentina looked tiny and frail under the starched sheets, wires relaying information that resulted in the reassuring, steady beep of the machines. Sofia felt tears start up again. She couldn't help it as she stared down at her mother, looking so helpless, so unlike herself. Her mother's eyes fluttered open, focusing as she registered her daughter and a wan smile appearing.

'What's this, Sofia? Tears?' she asked. 'Marinos don't cry.' Sofia laughed and nodded, brushing the tears off her cheeks with the back of her hand and stifling a sob.

'I have someone to see you,' Sofia said, looking down fondly, giving the arm resting on the sheet a stroke before stepping back to reveal Joey. Valentina's eyes widened in shock. 'Joey,' she breathed, 'I didn't think I'd see you again!'

'Having a heart attack was one way to bring me home,' he said gruffly, leaning in and carefully giving her a hug and kissing her cheeks. 'You always were one for drama, Valentina,' he joked, furtively rubbing his eyes.

'Mamma, I thought you said Marinos don't cry,' Sofia said, laughing with relief that her mother looked to be doing well.

'I'm sorry, Sofia,' Valentina said, grasping her daughter's hand, 'I didn't mean to spoil your trip.'

'Don't be ridiculous, Mamma, it wasn't going that well anyway,' said Sofia, thinking about Adam and wondering how he was. With a start, she realised that she hadn't told him where she was. They had jumped straight off the helicopter and taken the first connecting flight they could find, via Athens this time. Her only thought was getting home and praying she wouldn't be too late. She would never have been able to forgive herself if something had happened before she got back.

This thought made tears well up again. 'I'm just going to get us some coffee,' she said as brightly as she could, and went out into the hall to find the café. As she was waiting to be served, she emailed Peter. She couldn't deal with Adam right now. He'd be furious with her, and rightly so.

Relieved to see an instant response, she smiled at Peter's kind words of encouragement and well wishes. He was such a lovely boss; she was lucky to work with him. Taking the coffees back to her mother's room, she found the hallway had filled up with the rest of the brood and she spotted Suzie, arm wrapped firmly around Aldo's waist.

'Anything you two have to tell me?' she grinned. They both blushed and glanced at each other adoringly. 'You don't mind, do ya?' Suzie asked, a look of concern clouding her face.

'Mind? I'm thrilled.' Sofia gushed, 'I couldn't ask for a better sister-in-law!'

'Steady on, Piccolo,' Aldo said but looked pleased.

'I'm just going to take this coffee in to Zio Joey,' Sofia said, then I will leave them to catch up and we can do the same.

The conversation halted abruptly when she walked back into the room, they obviously had things they wanted to discuss. 'I'll just leave this here,' Sofia said, placing the paper cup on the nightstand.

'Thank you, Sofia,' Joey said, 'do you mind if I have some time to catch up with your ma?'

Slightly puzzled by the secrecy, but eager to speak to Suzie, she replied, 'of course, take all the time you need. I will be just out here, Mamma.'

☼

Adam was woken up the next morning by the sunlight streaming through the window of what had turned out to be one of six bedrooms in the restored farmhouse. He and Anna had sat talking late into the night, almost finishing off the bottle of brandy, and his pounding head this morning was a sharp reminder. He wanted to shower but decided to hold off until he got back to the other apartment and could put on clean clothes, but was thankful to find an unopened toothbrush in the guest bathroom which went some way to remove the sour aftertaste in his mouth.

He went downstairs to find the kitchen and much-needed coffee, and discovered Maria already in there, preparing breakfast. His stomach growled, reminding him he hadn't eaten much the day before, and he gratefully accepted her offer of scrambled eggs and poured himself a large mug of coffee. Anna strolled in shortly after, looking bright and unaffected by their late night.

'Good morning, Adam, I hope you slept well?' she asked as she retrieved a mug from the cupboard and poured her coffee, adding a splash of cream before stirring it.

'I did, thank you. Sorry to keep you up so late last night,' he said, 'it was good to talk to someone about my situation with Sofia.'

She smiled over her cup at him, 'I understand, you must have been terrified thinking she was caught up in some underworld crime family!' She laughed, and Adam grinned sheepishly. How could he have been so stupid? He knew the fault for that lay firmly at his father's door, and maybe it was time Jack found a new hobby.

They took their breakfast out onto the terrace that looked over the rolling hills, and Adam felt himself coming back to life as he ate and they chatted about the plan for this morning. Anna was going to follow in her car as he drove back to Florence and between them, they would pack Sofia's suitcase. Anna would take it to the luggage forwarding company and he would take charge of the violin.

'So, what are you going to do about Sofia when you get back?' Anna asked him.

'Well, I will have to go and see her, I guess,' he said as he finished his eggs and placed his cutlery neatly on the plate. 'I don't know if she'll listen to me but I have to try.'

'Definitely!' Anna said. 'If you really love this girl, and it sounds to me like you do, you must do everything in your power to win her back. Take it from me; life is too short to ignore such things.'

Back at the apartment, he looked around with fresh eyes now he knew Joey wasn't a gangster. Maybe it would be a good option for Sublime Retreats? He shook his head. He couldn't think about it now, it would have to wait until he got back to Houston. Anna made quick work of collecting Sophia's things together and the suitcase was soon packed and standing by the front door. She came out of the bedroom holding up the violin case, 'here it is, I found it in the wardrobe.'

She placed it on the table and clicked it open, both of them gazing at it in wonder. It was a beautiful object, even if you didn't know its value. Adam had done a quick search and had been blown away by the recent auction prices. The thought of being responsible for it on the way home was nerve-wracking. After Anna left, he collected his things together and called Andrea to let him know that he was leaving early, but would be in touch with a decision about the properties they had seen. Taking one last look around to make sure he hadn't forgotten anything, he picked up his case and the violin and went down to meet the taxi booked to take him to the airport.

MANGIA BENE, RIDI SPESSO, AMA MOLTO

(Eat well, laugh often, love much)

Sofia was sitting by her mother's bedside, chatting about the trip to Florence and the amazing things she had seen there.

'Mamma, it is wonderful there, you should go. Once you are better and out of here, you and Papa should plan a trip. I know Zio Joey would love it if you did.'

Her mother smiled at the thought, 'you may be right, Piccolo. It has been too many years since we went anywhere; we've always been too busy at the restaurant.'

'Well, I think Papa might be able to let go a little now. Aldo and the boys have been doing such a great job; he could be convinced to leave for a week or two.'

Valentina looked at her daughter seriously and said suddenly, 'were you planning to tell me what happened with you and this Adam?' Sofia flushed; she had tried to avoid thinking about him, let alone talking about him.

'I know something went on,' Valentina continued. 'I can see it in your eyes.'

Sophia shifted in her seat, not sure where to start. 'We... We fell in love,' she said simply, looking out the window. 'But it wasn't enough, we're two very different people at the end of the day and it would never have lasted. It's better it fizzled out quickly.' She turned back to look at her mother, silent tears rolling down her cheeks.

'Oh, sweetheart, I'm sorry.' She said, patting her arm, 'are you sure it's over?'

Sofia nodded miserably. She had to accept how things were, as hard as it was going to be.

'Well, you never know how things will work out, everything happens for a reason.' Valentina said sagely.

'If my grandmother had wheels, she'd be a bike!' Sofia snapped, immediately looking contrite. 'Sorry, Mamma, it's tough is all. I really thought we had something...' she trailed off.

'Well, maybe it is something worth fighting for, huh? I had to do some pretty crazy things to make things work when I met your father. My family hated his; he had no money, no prospects. It was me who worked at it. I did what needed to be done so we could have a life together. The restaurant, our families accepting us; it was my actions that pulled it together.' She stared off, lost in thought. It was hard for Sophia to imagine her mother as anything else but this calm, implacable woman who kept the family together with a combination of love, strength, and food.

Valentina snapped back to the present. 'Anyway, you should go. You said you would help at the restaurant while Aldo takes Suzie out for a while, so get to it, girl!'

Valentina dozed off again after Sofia left, dreaming of days gone by and the adventures of her youth. When she came to, a young man was hovering in the doorway. She didn't know him, but taking in his handsome features, worried expression and the nervously clutched violin, it didn't take much working out.

'Adam?' she asked croakily, trying to sit up and reach the glass of water on her bedside table. He immediately put the case on a chair, walked over to the bed, helped her sit up and passed her the glass.

'I'm sorry to disturb you, Mrs Marino, I was looking for Sophia.' He said, watching her take thirsty gulps. When she was sated, she put the glass back and said with a snort, 'I figured you weren't here to visit a fragile old woman!' He could see where Sofia got her sass and her looks from. Despite her pale countenance, when she smiled, the room lit up and he felt more confident. He had been worried sick that the entire family would be there and he would have to get past her brothers.

'I'm afraid you missed her, she's gone to the restaurant.' Valentina continued examining his face, looking to see what had captured Sofia's heart so suddenly. He pushed his glasses back on his nose and gave a nervous smile.

'Ah, I see. I just wanted to bring her that,' he said, pointing to the case. 'Can I leave it with you?'

Valentina continued to scrutinise him and seemed to reach a decision. 'No, I don't think you can. I think you need to take that case and your sorry ass to Margarita's and tell my daughter how you really feel about her.' Surprised at her vehemence, he stepped back, staring at her. 'And let me tell you something else, young man,' she said quietly, beckoning him closer. He took a tentative step towards her, sensing something dangerous. A hand with a vice-like grip whipped out and held his forearm, and he looked at it in surprise. She pulled herself towards him and hissed, 'if you ever, ever upset that girl again, I swear to God you will regret the day you were born, *capisce*?'

He looked into her eyes, which were so like Sofia's, yet there was something hard in there, something that reminded him of a shark. He felt something click into place and despite his fear he said, 'tell me something. Did you know your husband's family well? You know, back in the day?'

He saw a slight widening of her eyes before she pulled her face back under control and she released his arm with a low chuckle. 'You'll do, Son, you'll do,' she said before a coughing fit took over. He passed her the water again and waited until she could breathe normally, rubbing his arm and the imprint left there. She smiled again, like the sun appearing through the clouds. 'Now take those *cojones* of yours to our restaurant and if you can make it past my boys, you may have half a chance with Sofia.'

Adam went to push it, ask the question again, but thought better of it, and just said 'Yes, Ma'am,' picking up the violin and leaving, closing the door carefully behind him.

☼

Sofia was in the kitchen plating up orders when Fabio walked in and called over to her. 'Hey, Sis, there's some *Gonzo* out front asking for you, says he works with you?'

'Adam,' she breathed, shocked. She wasn't expecting to have to deal with him yet and her heart started pounding.

'You want me to give him the boot?' Fabio asked, pulling back his shoulders and his usual sunny demeanour slipping away, leaving a hard mask in its place.

'No, no, it's OK,' she said, quickly wiping her hands and pulling off her apron. The last thing she needed was her brothers Grimm going all Sicilian on him. She stood on tip-toes and peered through the glass of the kitchen doors, spotting him standing by the front door of the restaurant, looking completely out of place. Taking a deep breath, she strode out. Being on her home turf gave her confidence.

'Adam,' she said curtly, then, spotting the violin 'oh thank God, thank you for bringing that. You didn't need to come all the way over here!'

'I stopped by the hospital; your ma suggested it would be a good idea,' he said, a chastened look fleeting across his face. Sofia could just imagine her mother's reaction to his arrival. Feeling new respect for him, she smiled. He moved out of the way of another family arriving to eat and looked around.

'Nice place you have here,' he said tentatively.

'Thanks... Look we're kinda busy right now,' she stopped, a thought occurring 'what are you doing here? I mean, why aren't you still in Florence completing the deal for the apartment?'

'I couldn't just carry on knowing what you were going through, Sofia. I've been there, and I wanted to be here for you. Although I think it's safe to say your ma is on the road to recovery,' he chortled.

Sofia was in turmoil. She desperately wanted to throw herself into his arms and feel them holding her. She'd missed him dreadfully throughout the drama of the last 48 hours and wanted nothing more than to find the comfort that she knew was waiting there for her. Steeling herself to be strong, she said, 'Listen, Adam, it was lovely of you to come but I think you and I both know that we are better off returning to a working relationship.'

Aware that two of her brothers were loitering nearby, pretending to wipe down tables whilst they eavesdropped, he leaned in closer until he could smell the jasmine and said quietly, 'we need to talk, Sofia.'

'I'm not sure there's any point,' Sophia said rapidly, stepping back, causing Luca and Flavio to stand up straight, openly staring at them now. Sadly, Adam handed her the violin. 'Well, I think there is. You know where to find me if you change your mind.'

'Everything OK here?' a voice behind him said, and he whipped around, coming face to chest with Aldo, who was looking down on him like he was gum on the bottom of his shoe.

'Everything is fine, Aldo,' Sofia said hurriedly, pushing Adam's chest with her hand to get him to move towards the door. Taking his cue, he gave her a last, small smile and walked out of the restaurant. Sofia and Aldo watched him walk down the street and get into his car, Aldo with a scowl on his face, Sofia looking sad and a tear rolling down her cheek.

'You OK, Piccolo?' he asked, turning and taking in her expression.

'All good!' she replied too brightly 'he just came to bring the violin Zio Joey gave me' she said, holding up the evidence. Aldo nodded, disbelief writ across his face, but said, 'Alright. Let's get on with serving these people, shall we?'

Relieved, Sofia scarpered back into the kitchen, putting the violin on the desk and tying the apron back on. Her mind was racing. He'd flown back! Adam, who thought nothing was more important than his work, had flown back to be with her because he thought she needed support, abandoning his all-consuming mission to find the perfect apartment just for her. "Remember what a jackass he is," said the devil's advocate on her shoulder, "Remember how he treated you!" "But he came back for you," whispered the butterfly of hope that had settled firmly on the other side. Round and round the battle raged while she robotically went through the motions of plating up meals for the hungry hoards that had descended for lunch.

☼

On his drive home, Adam debated sending Peter an email but took the bull by the horns and called his boss to let him know that he had probably screwed things up in Florence by not closing the deal. He tapped his phone, resting the hands-free on the dashboard, and speed dialled the number.

'Hi, Adam, how're things going?' Peter asked when he picked up. 'Have we got our flagship City Breaks property?'

'That's why I'm calling, Peter. I'm sorry, but I came back before closing the deal. I came back for Sofia.'

There was a low laugh at the other end of the line. 'Well, it seems like I owe Annette five dollars. She said something was going on between you two!'

'I thought you'd be furious,' Adam said in confusion. The idea that he'd screwed up his career had been a close second to his dismay at screwing things up with Sofia.

'You know, I used to be just like you,' Peter's voice came through after a moment. 'I had nothing in my life except work; it was the only thing that I cared about. Then one day, Marc came to stay in one of our villas and I finally found true meaning in life. To love and share your life with someone who loves you equally is the greatest thing, the only thing that matters.'

Staring stiffly at the road ahead, Adam replied, 'Well I've blown that too. I was an idiot... For all sorts of reasons, and she wants nothing to do with me now.'

'Adam Flynn, where is the tenacity that I've always admired in you? I have never known you to give up on something once you've set your mind to it. If you want Sofia, go get her and don't give up until you do!'

Seeing an exit sign whizz by, Adam signalled and pulled over into the correct lane. 'Yes, boss!' he said with a grin and pulled off the highway, looped back around, and set course once again for Galveston.

☼

When the shift was finally over, the Marino brood sat around their usual table, eating some leftovers, discussing how the day had gone. Sofia picked at her food, not adding much to the conversation and by degrees, they picked up on her mood and a silence fell across the table. Aldo finally broke it. 'I guess you like this guy, huh, Piccolo?'

She looked up at him and saw all five of them staring at her. 'I do... I did. But it doesn't matter, it wouldn't work. We are two very different people.'

'Different isn't always bad,' Aldo responded. 'Look at me and Suzie!'

She gave him a soft smile, full of affection. 'You two have known each other since we were kids. It's a different scenario. And you don't have to contend with her having brothers!' she added, trying to lighten the mood.

'You know we'd support you if you loved this guy. You've just never shown an interest in anyone before.' He said, looking around the table for support, his brothers nodding in agreement. She gave a small shake of her head, 'that's good to know, but for now, let me show you the violin Zio Joey gave me, it's beautiful!'

Hoping that that was the end of the discussion, she ran to the desk in the kitchen and brought it out to the table. Fabio stacked the plates to one side so she could put it down and they all looked on in anticipation as she clicked open the case. There, resting on the top, was a velvet drawstring bag, its deep purple evoking opulence. She snatched it up and pulled it open, tipping the contents into her palm.

'What is it, Piccolo?' asked Roberto, peering over her shoulder. She gently held the clasp and dangled the intricately engraved heart so they could all see it. Eyes shining, she looked up. 'It's a charm for my bracelet,' she said in awe, 'look, it's a heart with a violin carved onto it.' She noticed a slip of paper still in the jewellery bag and pulled it out and read the two words written on it. "Forgive me."

She sat up, looking straight ahead, thoughts soaring, butterfly wings now firmly entrenched in her stomach. Standing up decisively he said, 'excuse me boys, there's someone I need to talk to', grabbing her bag from behind the bar and running to the door. She sped into the street, searching for her car keys in her bag, and ran slap bang into Adam.

They both reeled from the impact and the shock. Adam regained his composure first. 'Sofia, I couldn't just leave things like this,' he said, gazing down into her beautiful face. She looked up at him, thirstily taking in every line and contour before stretching up to place the sweetest kiss on his lips. He responded hungrily, wrapping his arms around her and lifting her off her feet as the spark that had appeared when they first met burst into a flame.

When they pulled apart, she smiled that smile and his heart was bursting with joy as she took his hand. 'Well, Adam, I think the time has come for you to meet my brothers,' she said, eyes glinting with mirth. 'Are you ready for this?'

He laughed, the sound ringing down the street. 'Ready as I'll ever be,' he said bravely, and she led him into the restaurant to meet her family.

FELICE PER SEMPRE

(Happy ever after)

Sofia nodded her thanks to Stefano as he placed the main course in front of her and looked around the table at her family and friends. Dressed in their finest, they were all relaxing now after the ceremony in the small church Zio Joey had arranged, chattering away excitedly. She felt her hand being squeezed and looked at Adam, sitting proudly beside her in his suit.

'You happy?' he asked quietly, leaning in close to her ear. His breath caused a shiver of excitement to run through her. A year later and the spark was still there. 'Never been happier,' she said and kissed him until the catcalls and whoops from around the table made her laugh and pull away.

Peter stood up, tapping his glass with a spoon to call their attention. Once the hubbub died down, he began, 'A toast to the happy couple – Adam and Sofia.' He turned and smiled at them proudly, 'I know you've had your ups and downs but I couldn't be happier to be here today, acting as your best man, Adam.' He waved his glass at him and Adam bowed his head in acknowledgement. 'I'm even happier to be here with Marc. Who knew on that dreadful day when I received the call that he had been in an accident that we would all be in Florence today, wishing this beautiful couple a long and happy life together.'

There was a round of applause and hands stretched out to pick up champagne flutes, which were raised in salute before drinking. Sofia was on cloud nine. She had never believed she would return to Florence when she left, but her insistence that she would not get married without Zio Joey and his love, Anna, had made them rethink all their plans. She took in Suzie and Aldo, heads together as always, laughing at some inside joke. Her Ma and Papa looking healthier and more vibrant; stepping back from running the restaurant after Valentina's heart attack had been the best thing in the world for them and her brothers had flourished. The restaurant was busier than ever.

Adam, who had been looking over at Jack to make sure he was doing OK, flinched when he felt a firm hand on his shoulder and looked up to see Aldo standing behind him. 'I did not expect to be welcoming this man into our family' his voice boomed over the table, 'but here we are, and I must say I could be getting a worse brother-in-law,' he added to a burst of laughter from his audience. 'But now, Adam, there is something I need to do,' and he brought a large, vicious-looking knife from behind his back and lent down over Adam's shoulder and grasped his tie.

'*Tagliodellacravatta!*' he shouted and in one swift movement brought the knife up to the knot and sliced through the fabric, holding the remnant aloft for all to see. Jack, who'd jumped up with an anguished cry, sank slowly back into his seat and downed the wine left in his glass. He was relieved that Adam was so happy now; the difference in him since he had met Sofia was plain to see. "But I will never get used to these crazy people," he thought, motioning to a waiter for more wine to settle his nerves.

When Adam had announced that he and Sofia were going to be married, Jack had been beside himself. He had, of course, met Sofia by then and he genuinely liked the girl, but he was still convinced that her family was bad news and the thought of his son getting caught up in anything shady terrified him. The conversation had not gone well and ended with Adam storming out of the house and not speaking to him for a week.

But Saturday rolled around and Adam reappeared, sheepishly, at the front door with a bag of his favourite snacks as a peace offering. They had sat and talked over the game and he convinced Jack to come and meet the family the next day at the restaurant and begrudgingly he had gone. Over the course of the fantastic meal that Valentina served, he had got to know them a little, but something still felt off to the cop in him, despite finding absolutely no evidence against Giovanni, no matter how hard he looked.

Anna interrupted his musings, pulling up the chair next to him. She smiled at him, 'you're not entirely comfortable are you Jack?' she queried with a glance around the table. Here was reason number two for his discomfort. The fact that this agent who had been declared dead years ago was alive and well and living the high life in Italy didn't sit well with him, even though he now knew the full story.

He gave a mirthless chuckle 'that's putting it mildly,' he replied, taking a sip of wine. 'But what can I do? Look how happy he is.' He gestured across the table to Adam, who was laughing out loud at something Sofia had said.

'That's all that counts, don't you think? Living well and being happy is ultimately what we all strive for.'

He nodded, not looking entirely convinced. She leaned in closer. 'What if I could guarantee you that Sofia's dad has never, in any way, been involved in a crime?'

He looked at her in surprise. 'That's a mighty big statement.'

'It is, but one that I know to be absolutely true, and I thought you might find a little peace from it,' she said seriously, studying his eyes for a response. 'Let this go, Jack. I'm sure there are plenty of other cold cases you could investigate; but even better than that,' she paused and pulled a business card out of her purse and slid it across the table. 'My friend back in Houston is looking for someone to head up his security team across the offices he manages. He particularly is looking for ex-police enforcement officers. I told him all about you and he is very keen to have a meeting when you get back.'

Jack looked down at the card on the table and slowly reached out a hand to pick it up, his mind racing. 'I'm not sure he wants an old codger like me,' he said, looking at it with a gleam in his eye.

'An old codger like you is exactly what he is looking for, Jack. Experienced, level-headed, and like a dog with a bone when it comes to details. You're a perfect fit.'

Looking up, he saw Adam was staring at him and saw him nod, encouraging him. He grinned in response before tucking the card into his pocket and saying to Anna, 'well I'll certainly give it some thought.'

Adam, happy that his father might have a new reason to get up in the mornings that had nothing to do with researching family connections, looked across at Valentina, who gave an imperceptible nod. It had been her idea to find Jack something else to do, and she had also suggested it best came from Anna. He had to give her credit. She certainly knew how to control the men around her. There was a loud fanfare as they wheeled the cake in on a trolley that could barely support its weight. Sofia squealed and pulled him to his feet to take their place centre stage and cut the monstrosity.

As they leaned into each other for the photographer to take his shots, he whispered in her ear, 'what do you say, Mrs Flynn, shall we sneak upstairs and consummate our marriage?'

She laughed out loud, throwing her head back in delight before replying sotto voiced, 'You know full well, Mr Flynn that we have members staying in the apartment upstairs. You will have to wait until we get to our hotel.' They turned sideways on, following the directions of the photographer, and he muttered, 'I was thinking of somewhere a little higher up? For old times' sake?'

Sofia felt a thrill run through her and knew she was blushing violently, but nonetheless turned her head slightly and nodded. When they snuck out an hour later, they ran hand in hand as fast as they could up to the roof, Sofia holding up the hem of her dress to avoid tripping up the stairs, and they burst through the door at the top giggling like schoolchildren. The air was a crisp relief after the heat and the noise of the restaurant and he pulled her into his arms, swinging her around before kissing her deeply.

'So this is where it all began,' he said, gazing down at her.

'I'd like to think it began a little before you saw me naked for the first time,' she teased.

He kissed her again. 'Well, let's agree that now is the beginning of a long, happy life together?'

She reached up and touched his cheek gently, the smile he loved so much blazing from her face. 'Well, it had better be Mr Flynn. If not, my mother might just have to kill you…' she said, stretching up to silence him with a kiss.

Printed in Great Britain
by Amazon